THE DRAMATURGICAL METAPHOR

A novella

THE DRAMATURGICAL METAPHOR

A novella

KEN CHAMPION

First published August 2014

© Ken Champion

The author asserts his moral right to be identified as the author of the work.

All rights reserved. No part of this publication may be reproduced, stored in a retrieval system or transmitted in any form or by any means, electronic, mechanical, photocopying, recording or otherwise, without the prior permission of the publishers

ISBN 978-1-291-97565-9

Cover: Rue Racine, Paris 1967 – photo by Ken Clay

PENNILESS PRESS PUBLICATIONS
Website : www.pennilesspress.co.uk/books

For
Steve, Tim & Toby

Reviews of previous fiction:

URBAN NARRATIVES

'I thank him for gracing our magazine with his literature… his realism is enriched with imagination, the most real of all qualities.'

Meredith Sue Willis, Hamilton Stone Review ('14)

'From the poignant first story, 'Art House,' and the inventively funny yet sad 'Verstehen,' through to the gritty realism of the urban college stories and the often bedevilled clients of a flawed East London analyst, I think his work is amazing.'

Sarah Katharina Kayß, The Transnational Magazine ('14)

'Ken Champion seeks out situations and characters that, though true to life, are different. He describes them with directness and freshness, weaving story lines which flow through settings that have connotations of both the cameo and the epic. The visual descriptions reflect the author's analytical voice which becomes a unique trademark. It all makes for a great read.'

Juli Janna ('14)

'I've been a fan of Ken Champion's work for quite a while now. He writes with empathy and honesty and includes more than a touch of dark humour. The compelling descriptions of urban landscapes ground the restlessness, defiance and unpredictability of the characters and allow him to explore the themes of, amongst many others, relationships and death.

'She in a department store, disappearing, and him unguarded, panicking, intellectually knowing that it was the child in him being left by mummy - no emotions are new.' *(Fracture)*
The beauty of a short story is that it doesn't have to tie up every loose end and several of the stories contain coincidences that eave us wondering. They often contain hard truths.

'The equation being that if he looked fit and tanned then he wouldn't age, ergo, wouldn't die. It was a subject he'd never studied: the psychology of death.' *(Lay Preacher)*
I'm already looking forward to his next publication.'

Joanna Ezekiel ('14)

CHAPTER 1

'Keep yer 'at on, they're sackin' the old uns.'

The voice from his artisan past - a foreman's jocular advice to a balding chippie as one of the governors came on site - was triggered by the tonsorially challenged man in the Rive Gauche bookshop he was passing on his way to Pont Saint-Michel to meet a client. As he walked, he was looking across to the Rive Droite, above which were geometric contrails in the sky noughts and crosses could have been played on. He'd caught the train from Charles de Gaulle to the Gar du Nord's metro line to Paris Saint-Germain, dropped his bag off at a small hotel tucked behind the grander ones and thought about the first time he'd left England and had come to this city.

He was eighteen and remembered stepping off the coach from Calais at Abbeville and negotiating the French language and national currency successfully enough to order some chips, a choc ice and a packet of *Gauloises.* For someone halfway through a manual apprenticeship he'd felt thrilled that his request had been understood. The excitement had been dampened when he and his friend's east London accents were mocked by their Chanel-groomed tour guide. 'Cockney sparrows' she'd called them in her luscious French cadence.

The last time he had been here was with his late brother, the image of him now immediately morphing into a thousand others as he approached Pont de la Tournelle and watched the Seine moving quietly and aristocratically beneath it. Hearing jazz music - that individualistic self expression of the middle classes and their erroneous assumption of a meritocratic world - from a café across the street, he was conversely reminded of the entrenched fatalism of his own early culture and a family tale of a grandparent who had refused to go into an air raid shelter during the London blitz, saying smugly that, 'If Jerry's bombs ain't got my number on 'em I'll be alright.' and walking about the streets as if he was going for an evening stroll before the pub. James recalled him occasionally saying, in First World War Tommy French, 'Parlay voo mamzell, lah prominard,' and his wife smiling proudly up at him.

He crossed the road, went inside and, while waiting for a coffee, ran through a mental list of things he liked about Paris other than its cleanliness and order, tree-lined boulevards, symmetrical aesthetic, slim women and insistence on salad with everything. The lack of graffiti, fly posting, advertising hoardings, music vibrating from cars, narcissistic, architectural deformities - here, new buildings often mimicked the old - and the paucity of American influence. What he enjoyed most, at a more satisfying level, was the normative protection the country's culture seemed to provide against the rest of the world.

But he was aware that all this was a deflection. Here, now, was a world apart from that, apart from his brother, family and often misshaped nostalgia. He was James Kent, psychoanalyst, and in another forty minutes would be beginning something he had been trying to rationalise, downplay in an attempt to push away uncertainty and feelings of professional immorality by calling what he was going to begin, just another job.

He had never met anyone from the psychotherapeutic practice that had contacted him, but was aware that it was a leading organisation in the symbolic universe to which he belonged. He had, it seemed, been suggested to them by a colleague. He'd been met in its sleek, tropical plant-potted, Pollock print office by a thin, humourless man who had taken him to a restaurant in Charlotte Street where, after pointless small talk that was a waste of the human ability to speak, had got to the matter in hand.

'Sorry to be mysterious about this, but the practice, I'm a small part of it, really, has been funded a rather large amount for research. As you've told me, you have time on your hands and that's exactly what's needed; someone who can commit, with skills that are less conducive to number crunching than they are to pragmatic analysis and, hopefully, able to be utilised in environments other than a consulting room. This could well be twenty four seven if you take it. It is, I suppose, rather a strange request.'

CHAPTER ONE

'There's a rich client of the senior partner who wants someone, a therapist, to be with him all of the time, I'm sure your immediate thought, as was mine, is that such ultra dependency would be bad for him, counter-productive. I'm more preaching to the converted here than teaching a grandmother to suck eggs, but in the end he has to do the work, it's down to him, isn't it and, to pre-empt you again, I'm guessing that you're thinking you'll become too involved; from a non-participating observer to a non-observing participant, perhaps. He seems to want not so much a body guard as a kind of ego guard, a - '

'Mother, he wants a mummy.'

'Well, maybe, but I'm sure - '

'That I won't protect him needlessly?'

'Of course. The partner has seen him just the once, I think, but when the research funding was offered, instead of the usual mid-scale head counting, info gathering, he thought that a close-up study would be more useful.'

'Very close up. It seems strange to fund something involving someone who is so well off. I know it's in the name of research, but there are surely more deserving cases to spend this money on. How does your partner justify the funding?'

'Leave that to him. And, by the way, the client's happy to pay all over-and-above expenses, apparently.'

'I'm wondering if your colleague sees this as a bit of a gamble. I don't want to play dice with a man's health. I'm wondering, also, what the client sees it as; an adventure perhaps, maybe he's bored or wants to exercise his power, wants someone to run around for him, always be there, a lackey.'

'I imagine he has enough money to have that any time he chooses.'

James told him he needed time to think about this rather dubious, potentially conflicting proposal.

'Of course, I understand your hesitation. But, maybe, just maybe, he really is desperate.' He signalled to the waiter, paid the bill and said, 'Don't leave it too long though, will you.'

He went home and upstairs to the study where he looked at his practice file: income for the last six months, outgoings, patient list, tax... He put it away. He knew how little money he had as well as its potential scarcity in the immediate future. Perhaps he'd already made his decision, but he couldn't imagine listening to someone, treating them away from this room and its pale green walls, leather couch, sanded pine floorboards and his framed diplomas. He looked through the room's box sash window at the courtyard garden, past the scruffy tree to the backs of the Victorian houses in the next street and thought that maybe he was in a career rut, a little too used to the consistently fraught, awkward relationships played out in this familiar terrace cottage on which he still owed years of mortgage repayments.

He felt annoyed with this man who he had never met and knew so little about. Was he a spoilt child used to wealth and an unthinking sense of entitlement, to sycophants, supplicants and wanting to add another? His request appeared to be for an enforced relationship based on one person's money and another's - James disliked admitting it - relative poverty. He looked through his window again and recognised in the murkiness of an early dusk the beginning of a wallow in something like self-pity. He picked up a book on existentialism he'd recently added to his shelves, Camus providing the opening lines. 'There is but one truly serous philosophical problem and that is suicide. Judging whether life is or is not worth living amounts to answering the fundamental question of philosophy.' It went downhill from there.

He rang his interviewer again the next morning and asked when he could meet the senior partner.

'It's really a case of whether rather than when, he's very busy with - '

'No. When.'

'I've been told that you may meet the customer, we can arrange something.'

''May' meet him? 'Customer'?'

'Sorry, management speak,'

'He needs to contact me.'

'I'll tell him.'

It was a pleasantly English accent that conveyed its owner's charm to James next day over the phone; it also held, in the few sentences spoken, a reluctance to fully inform.

CHAPTER ONE

James considered a moment. 'I feel that you'd like me take this job - ' 'Carry out the research,' the senior partner's voice interrupted, 'based on a few rather grudgingly given words. I need more than this.'

'My time's limited. I'm emailing you a summary of my notes now. You'll have the basics. You'll receive a letter shortly detailing your fee, its terms, expenses, etcetera. I do hope you'll accept. Mister Lewis, the man you met, will forward your number to the client. His name is Lazen. Good day.'

James went into his study. The email was already there.

Re. The Client.

The present for him appears to be fraught with internal difficulties, partly manifested in a restlessness; always wanting to be where he's not, not wanting to be where he is. He can afford to follow this urge. I am not sure whether I can add much to this. I've met him just the once, two weeks ago. The week preceding this meting he had travelled to Berlin and Palermo and was intending to visit Sofia.

J.W. Morgan.
Morgan, Bayer and Partners

Knowing there was little choice and to save himself from further procrastination James responded with his acceptance. Picking up his book again he read Heidegger's question regarding thought, 'Where is thought *in* the world?' Perhaps, he mused, we can only infer that a thought exists, like causality or god they weren't amenable to sense data. But then, positivism, like religion and magic, is a self contained conceptual system that can, in itself, be neither right nor wrong, that can... The phone rang.

It was a rather rushed, but not unpleasant voice, carrying words which, James felt, had been carefully considered yet were rather vague in communicating what the speaker of them actually wished for. The short, one-sided conversation - all James had managed to say was, 'Yes, speaking.' - finished with, 'Now that you've heard me and, I assume haven't been put off, I'll email you when and where to meet.'

He'd rung off leaving James feeling that he was merely a passive receiver of information, a recipient of other people's wants and instructions.

He was leaning against the balustrade of the bridge looking across to the other bank and the river below. There was something clean and morally right about the grey-blue water of the Seine, unlike the sluggish brown of London's main river with its growing number of Lego developments on its banks as the city's packed inhabitants moved higher. He looked at the Ile de la Cite. at the Basilica's flying buttresses - part functional, part conceit - and then along a tree-edged boulevard that, narrowing to a fog of branches in the autumn afternoon, looked like a Utrillo of *fin de sèicle* Paris. He saw a horse, a grey, pulling a cab, a man crossing in front of it, jacket swirling in the wind, an obvious *poseur* standing on a pavement and an elderly *roué* apologising as he bumped into a woman with a long dress hanging below her coat.

He noticed, as he had before, how casually elegant the women who walked past him were, some even wearing hats, and with handbags swinging like small pendulums. Two children danced by holding hands, then a tall, well built figure wearing a fedora and a dark cape-like coat like an old Sandeman Sherry advert passed him. It stopped and turned

'Are you... ?'

The words came from a furrowed, but smooth face with wide cheekbones and full lips. He recognised the voice.

'I am.'

The man held out his hand. James shook it. He removed the hat, showing a large, enviably well shaped head with thick, greying hair, briefly wiped his brow with the back of a hand and suggested they have coffee. 'This way,' he smiled.

As James took a step to be level with him, he heard a voice calling.

'Karl.'

Across the other side of the bridge a taxi was slowing to a stop, part of a woman's face showing above a side window, the eyes

CHAPTER ONE

glancing quickly left and right. The door opened and a tall, curvaceous woman, sartorially at home with herself in a long, flowing dress, skipped smoothly towards them. As she stepped onto the pavement, she looked quickly behind her.

'I can't ask him to wait there. Ring me.'

She turned and hurried back to the taxi, smiling and waving at Lazen as it moved away. He looked steadily at the vehicle as it continued across the bridge and vanished into the traffic. He turned to James again and started walking.

'The Café Bleu's rather nice. We'll eat, too, if you're hungry.' James wasn't. 'Nice Journey? Fly? Eurostar? Ferry? It can be tiring, travelling, can it not? Though I suppose it's a function of how excited you are, how much one anticipates, savours the destination. Who was it said, 'It's neither the travelling nor arriving, it's the getting up and going.'? But there's always the rather boring, even nasty bits of journeying and…'

He went on, asking almost-questions, making inconsequential observations while James nodded absently and looked around him; a wide avenue ahead, neatly pruned trees, a corner café bar with its comfortably balanced ambience of artisans and bourgeois drinking alcohol and coffee, eating quiche and baguettes. They turned into a street and into a cafe at its end, Lazen leading the way. He continued with his ersatz stream of consciousness over coffee till James, bored with his own nodding contributions, raised his hands, palms outwards.

'Can you tell me exactly what you want of me?'

There was a long pause. 'I want you to be around me, observe me, see what you can make of my actions when I'm with people, when… try to understand me, somehow just help me. Of course you're supposed to analyse me, get to it all, though I don't know whether I can answer your questions truthfully; I do want to. I've booked you into the hotel, a room near mine. I don't know how long I, we, will be there, but don't worry about anything; all will be paid for, as you know. And, look, I need to go.' He smiled, reached into his pocket, pulled out a keycard and placed it on the table.

'Your room at the Petit Trianon. It's a simple place. I happen to like it.' He stood. 'See you soon.' He went towards the counter, stayed a moment then went out the door without looking back.

James kept where he was. Now that he'd met the man, felt a little of his personality, knew he was real, he wondered just how he could help him. He needed to be in an enclosed space with him, but this was a restless being in Paris who, perhaps, wouldn't want to stay in a room for more than a few minutes. He left, returned to the hotel where he'd dumped his bag and went to his new one.

He went through its heavy, ornate swing door, the foyer's scrolls and heavily embossed ceiling reminding him that Paris was a city built on empire, and up to his room. It was a spacious double one with black and pink Lilium wallpaper, marquetry inlaid writing table, a large baroque bed and a mirrored mahogany wardrobe. He felt that his clothes, himself, were inappropriate, neither should be here, it was too heavy, too grand.

After showering he walked back to the same café, mainly because Lazan had just been in there with him and he wanted to think about him. There was a Gaggia machine gurgling loudly, a waiter dressed like one in a Café Rouge and, instead of a large black and white photo of the Eiffel Tower or an aerial view of the Seine on the wall, there were pictures of the Houses of Parliament and Trafalgar Square. He didn't want the world's cities to be pictorially exchanged, Paris should be Paris, a city set in aspic, as a friend had once said to him. He wanted it to remain so.

There were few customers; his coffee served by an apron-less man who asked him if he was English.

'Does it show?. Using the longest French phrase he knew, he added, *'Je ne parle pas français, je suis desolé.'*

'It's alright, my English is good, I lived there for a while, I was chief patisserie cook at Brown's. I'll be moving back there shortly.'

James asked him where he was going.

'To east London, Wanstead, it's like a village, it's a shop in the High street, it already has a French name.'

'I know it, I live in the area, I occasionally gaze at its pictures of the Arc de Triomphe and a Dordogne farm house.

The man laughed, introduced himself as Fabian and said, *'Que le monde est petit,'* and talked of how much the patrons of

CHAPTER ONE

Brown's had loved his recipes for jam sponge and spotted 'deek.' He asked what James was doing in the city.

'Just meeting up with a friend, looking around.'

A customer entered. Fabian turned to go across to him, saying over his shoulder, 'I saw you with M'sieur Lazen a little while ago.'

After serving the newcomer, who was sitting in a far corner, he came over to James again, this time sitting down.

'He is your friend, yes?' James nodded. 'He occasionally comes here; he is very likeable, isn't he. I first saw him a few months ago with a girl, very attractive. It wasn't just her looks, but the way she dressed.' He exaggerated his accent, spread his arms and said with a grin, 'I am French, I notice these things, so *jeune et belle*. Do you mind me talking of him?' James shook his head. 'I then saw him about a month ago in a bar in Neuilly. There was a woman, sort of upper class, as you would say. She'd been sitting on her own. There were some admiring looks at her, including mine. He was at the bar and went across to her and he was obviously, er, chatting her up.' James increasingly liked the way casual English phrases were moulded by his accent. 'They were laughing. He walked out with her after a time. I was sure they'd never met before, but as he held the door for her I realised it was the girl I'd first seen him with. I'm not completely sure, but almost certain. It seemed strange. It's nothing to do with me, of course.'

As he gave his Gallic shrug again half a dozen people came in at once and he got up, leaving James to muse on his client. It seemed to him that everyone; the partner, the café owner, a woman - or two - probably the entire staff of the hotel knew him. He tried to establish what the game plan was, when he was supposed to see him again; he didn't know even that. He got up, caught Fabian's eye and walked back to the hotel.

It was getting dark, street lights were switching on, the last light of the sun glittering the river. It was the little bits of the city he liked, not so much the rococo, Napoleonic, the Place de l'Opera, but a Lavirotte building, the Coulee Verte, the metro entrances, while across a narrow street a lamp on the corner of a building illuminated an embracing couple.

He was dithering. Where his professionalism should be dominating it was indulgent visual images that were filling him. What ailed the man? Of course, he didn't *have* to sit him down and use his well practised techniques, his sometimes successful methods, perhaps he could play it by ear, theorise on the hoof, as it were. He tried to accept the inevitability of it and go back to his room and sleep. He did, the wallpaper pattern swirling through his dreams of auburn haired girls, taxis and chestnut trees.

In the morning he went down to a late breakfast in a room at the side of the restaurant, the guests, having already vacated, leaving their culinary remains to be cleared by a solitary waiter. Except one. Gazing down at a neatly folded *Paris Match* on a dining chair beside him was Lazen. He was wearing a grey blazer, dark trousers and a polo shirt. He gave his wide-lipped smile.

'Hello Mister Kent, do sit.'

As he did, James ritualistically slipped into friendly therapist mode. 'Perhaps 'James' would be better. If it's alright with you, that is.' He received a nod.

'Would you like to pretend this is a consulting room, say, my study, try to relax, talk to me?' James asked half seriously

Lazen looked at the ceiling then down again and took a deep breath. 'I'm running away, aren't I. All this,' He looked around, 'restaurants, hotels, flights,' He smiled, 'Me, fleeing; cities, Sofia, Istanbul, Brussels, Madrid - '

'Do you know what you're running away from?'

He looked at James with annoyance then continued. 'New York, of course, then Seattle I think it was; even a desert once.'

'Why did you go there, to yell in the wilderness?'

For a second his face held an odd expression; as if wanting to say yes, but unable to do so. He drew himself upright.

'Shall we go somewhere? I suppose I don't see as much as I should when I go to places, it's just the occasional concert, a gallery or something, but not to...'

'Parks, avenues, alleyways?'

'I suppose so. I don't walk much.'

They left the hotel, Lazen seemingly taking it as said that James would do so without breakfasting, and crossed the street. He was silent. James let him be and looked about him. It was the

CHAPTER ONE

sun on trees, on walls, flashing from a chimney cowl, a window; it was a form of spirituality. London again; Hampstead, Brakenbury village, Edwardes Square, a buttress on a Highbury church, a shop awning in Ealing; a soft focused, harsh, gentle, vivid montage of excitement, peace, of head-back laughter with his brother along Thames towpaths, canal bridges; a trunk load of feelings and experiences. But this was Paris, a French nostalgia, not as deeply felt as that of his own city, but there..

'Are you with me, Mister Kent, er, James?' Lazen spoke the last word as if it was one he had never used before.

'Yes. I was thinking.'

'Of a woman?'

'No, a city, What's your favourite city? Have you one?'

'I've never really considered it. The Hotel Cosmos in Moscow, Radisson Acron in Prague, Casa Del Mar in LA, I suppose. Of course, you asked me about cities, not the hotels. I guess I was right about my insular attitude to the urban world.' He shrugged. 'Should I extend my experiences outside of hotel rooms and bars a little more then?'

'There are no 'shoulds' here,' but I suppose I feel like being rather unprofessional and projecting my own interests on to you.'

They walked on, James noticing that Lazen would slow each foot a fraction before it left the ground, giving him, with his dark, greying hair long and swept almost horizontally at the back, the movement of an Italian aristocrat or a Fellini-created intellectual; the look of a man who, somehow, had psychological ownership of everything. For a moment James almost basked in his fascination of the man's own fabrication.

Neither spoke, the analyst allowing the client to follow his psyche's own internal rhythms; to speak when he wanted about what he wanted. But it was mostly inconsequential, though interesting: a visit to Niagara Falls and its unexpected commercialism, how huge and flat the Russian steppes were, traffic jams in Honolulu, and his fascination with a lone plume of smoke stretching for miles from a factory chimney as he came into land at Istanbul. James almost walked on past the bar that Lazen had half turned into.

'This do you? What you having?'

It was too early for James to drink. He settled for English breakfast tea and a baguette, his host having wine. It was a long, high ceiling place with few people present. Lazen took a large swig and smacked his lips.

'Look, Christ, I didn't think I'd be here telling someone this, I never have.' He took a deep breath, exhaled slowly.

'It doesn't matter what I call you does it, just… listen. I live in a kind of third person, I am continually, relentlessly watching myself, always, always, always.' He looked around him, clenching his teeth then tried to relax. 'I act all the time, *all* of the time. I feel I'm telling the truth, feeling what I think but, I'm acting even now and even as I say 'I'm acting even now,' I'm aware there's a detached part that's watching me, listening to me and watching that which is watching me. It doesn't matter how quickly I'm thinking, moving, how occupied I am, it's there; a kind of infinite regress of observing.' He looked at James with dark, anxious eyes. 'It rarely stops. Even now when I want to… feel, I see myself talking to you.' He paused. 'Perhaps, at this moment, I'm acting a man who has money and needs an analyst.' He stopped talking, looked down then out of the window and said quietly, 'I'm not really a person. I - '

'What are you then, a moose?'

Lazen forced a grin. 'I suppose that's rather profound, but I don't want to think about it now.' He continued gazing out the window.

James looked at the man's profile as the eyes watched the traffic outside. What he'd said raised the question of what and where his real, existential self was. This wasn't just the separation of the 'I' and 'me', the 'known' and the 'knower,' they were givens, reflexivity was a defining characteristic of being human; 'A horse is a body, we *have* a body' came from the first week of his undergraduate days. This was more than that.

Lazen turned towards his listener. '*I've* got to do this haven't I, you can't.' He looked quickly around him again. 'Look, I'm going.' He stood. 'It's on the tab. Eat the place up.' Moving towards the door, he flicked a hand in acknowledgement and walked away past the window.

James began mentally racing through psychological categories, constructs: bi-polar, paranoia... He stopped. A drive for a sort of hyper empathy welled in him for a moment, he wanted to *feel* this man, to get inside of him, to somehow thump him back to childhood and then clutch it away from him, holding it in his fist in front of his face, saying, 'This is it, this is *you.*' He looked at the café's end wall filled with a tromp l'oeil photograph of a Mediterranean house in the sun, wanting to be there, live in the room opening on to the balcony with its shaded walls, bright rugs, a fig tree in the corner of a Parma ham, carbonara laden kitchen and a Sylvana Mangano look-alike leaning back against the sink smiling at him while he occasionally came out and looked down at people grinning up, *Ciao, come stai. Come e Lucilla...* but not to be here with this man and wondering whether his own motive was to genuinely help him or to look at the imaginary contents of his fist and analyse what was there, dissect it for his own intellectual satisfaction. He felt a familiar spiritual dampening. He left the place and walked in the opposite direction to Lazen.

He strolled along a boulevard, not knowing its name nor really caring. Sometimes he preferred it this way, wherever he was, just looking around, finding little bits here, pieces there, sometimes seeing it as an analogy for the process with a patient; searching, uncovering a repressed nook here, covert cranny there. He looked up as a flash of evening sun illuminated a window - immediately resisting furthering his analogy by seeing the lit aperture as a window on the soul - and stopped outside a restaurant to watch early diners take their seats. He looked at the menu posted outside, most of which he couldn't understand. He knew he could probably order what he wanted and Lazen would pay. He was tempted to when he saw a waiter hurry to a table almost not balancing a tall croquembouch, one of the few desserts he'd heard of, ficelle and mille-feuilles being strangers, the main dishes being only a little more familiar. He couldn't bring himself to, he'd internalized the protestant ethic; he had to earn it.

After walking to and across the mossy green Pont Mirabeau, lunching on the Rive Droite and catching a metro back, he returned to the hotel. As he entered his room Lazen was behind him.

'May I come in?'

Without waiting for a reply he entered and sat. James stood looking at him.

'I mentioned you observing me partly as a change from me observing me. I want you to tomorrow in La Venus, it's a bar. I'll be with a friend, we do this occasionally, we... interplay. I'll approach her, but she doesn't know who or what I am, or I what her response will be, it's just a game. I enjoy it, it amuses me.'

James was silent.

'If you're thinking that it's because the idle rich have little better to do, you'd be wrong. I'd do this, anyway. I'll try not to be too aware that you're there, though I suppose it will alter the way I behave a little, You can sit nearby somewhere.'

'Do you want to show off?'

'Of course not.'

'I'm to be a voyeur then? What am I going to see?'

'You'll see a man looking just like me,' he smiled, 'approaching a woman who - '

'Not in third person, refer to yourself, feel it. And what do you hope to gain by me being here?'

'You may be able to find something, some things about me that I don't know of. Just watch me and tell me afterwards what you think.' He stood. 'Just come to the place, be there, about eight. It's a start, isn't it? A beginning?'

'Of what?'

'I don't know.' Enunciating the words slowly and clearly, he said, 'See you tomorrow.' He strode quickly from the room, not closing the door.

Next day, feeling lazy, James mostly rode around on the metro. There were few people in the carriages; no stink of hot meat pasties, no vaporous shouting into mobiles which, on his way to St. Pancras, had prompted him to point out to a passenger that as his communications device was electronically assisted he didn't have to shout all the way to Krakow. As his train smoothed along he idly wondered if foreigners' shouting was either a result of the genetic shape and tenseness of their vocal cords or culturally learnt; their bombast versus his English diffidence, then wondering where the latter had come from.   Perhaps the indigenous middle classes had been shaped thus when England

CHAPTER ONE

had supposedly ruled the world and there was, therefore, no need to raise their voices. He'd also watched in the same carriage a young man having his hair firmly grabbed by his laughing, older companion seated beside him, his head bent back and being kissed firmly and repeatedly on his lips. The passengers opposite had sat uncomfortably looking down at their newspapers, smart phones or at the floor. James heard himself inwardly saying, 'Fine, get married if you want, but don't spend your honeymoon on the fuckin' Central line.'

The La Venus bar was in a side street off Boulevard St. Germain. With its tiled ceiling mural, Lalique glass displayed behind the three sided mahogany bar, tiffany lighting, rococo mirrors and an accordionist playing quietly in a far corner. it was the quintessential French bar, almost, thought James, verging on twee. It was well occupied, but not crowded. He sat just inside the entrance and on a whim ordered absinthe, thinking of the 'absinthe makes the heart grow fonder' line and further reminded of it by an old advertising poster framed on a side wall showing a man seated at a café table with his chin resting in cupped hands and glancing up at a transparent nude, her arse on the table cloth, splayed fingers taking her weight and foot lightly touching the floor. Her profile and bobbed hair seemed to quietly insist that he didn't have to stay with a spiritually corseted wife, he'd only to sweep his financial papers and his life onto the parquet and she would be flesh again, his hand resting on the inside of her thigh, a chair and baroque lamp no longer seen through her waist. But it could be merely a businessman's reverie, something to think about till the waiter arrived bottle in hand, and at the edge of the picture there he was, foot slightly raised and James wondered whether his shoe would descend or rise and whether the girl would disappear as he came nearer or if he would casually ask after *m'sieur's* wife while looking past him at the Art Deco clock just visible outside.

His own reverie was halted as a woman entered. She was tall, with pale auburn hair, green eyes and a figure slightly fuller than most of the indigenous female population. It was the woman from the taxi on the bridge. She nodded to a barman and took a stool at the bar. He glanced at her legs; perhaps it was the instantly imagined combination of Bardot and old films with Charisse that triggered the early adolescent thrill. She didn't look around, appearing quite familiar with her surroundings and took a book from her bag and began to read.

Lazen, wearing an open-necked shirt and carrying a jacket over his shoulder with pseudo Gallic charm, came in on cue, walked by her stool then stopped and turned to her.

'Ilaria?'

'She looked up at him.

'Sorry, apologies,' he said, falsely contrite, 'you're so like her, this woman I know, it's almost uncanny, Again, I'm sorry. She's not quite as beautiful as you, though. Really.'

She gave him what James' mother would have called an 'old fashioned look.'

'It's true. It's also an innocent remark.'

Looking down at the vacant stool next to her as if he'd just noticed it he made a small gesture towards it. 'Do you mind if I sit next to you?' He sat, not waiting for a reply. He asked if she was waiting for someone then they began, disappointingly to James, speaking in French, he more fluent than she. James tried to guess what he was; he was displaying the smooth confidence of a rather period Riviera playboy. Whatever he was it was the epitome of effortless charm and however seemingly reluctant she was to be seduced there was an obviously un-faked pleasure in his company.

After a time they both got up and, while the woman put on her jacket, Lazen went to the bar and paid, then, escorting her in front of him as they walked towards the entrance, his face flushed, eyes alive, he surreptitiously winked at James as he held the door for his companion and they left. James wondered if he was expected to follow. He decided not to. He thought about where they may have met. Had he bought her?

When he returned to the hotel he went to his room, lay on the bed, arms behind his head and tried to sum up the last few hours. He was aware he was feeling rather angry and had been for a while. This was manifested in his impatience with the man, his brusqueness. He knew this client was full of escapes, deflections,

CHAPTER ONE

non sequiturs and, perhaps, was intelligent enough to say things which he knew would set James thinking of a theory, a direction, a piece of analysis that was erroneous, leading him up a garden path into a psychological thicket of thorns, his time wasted, Partly, he felt, it was because he wasn't at home surrounded by familiar objects, colours and possessions; here it was more his client's world, however, troubled it may be. When Lazen's mind wandered too near his problems he could buy something: drinks, a journey, a woman; his cash bought places to run to, people and things to run with and which were preventing confrontation with himself. James wondered how much, if any, intellectual recognition his client had of the genesis of his difficulties. What he was fairly certain of was that the pain of hiding it all was becoming almost as great as that which he was hiding. James guessed that this was why he had been invited here.

But perhaps he wasn't really the right man for this. He had to decide whether he was going to use the sum of his training, experience and knowledge to do the best he could or... There was no alternative now. He attempted to relax, tried to think that he should allow, even encourage his client not only to say what he wanted, but to do what he wanted, at least for now, and with gentler questioning from himself. Maybe he could even enjoy things while he was here. He placed an extra pillow under his head and went to sleep.

CHAPTER 2

As he got ready for breakfast next morning he managed to get Radio 4 on the room's radio. It was familiar, almost comforting, until the 'you knows' and 'I means' began - obsessively counting four of the former and two of the latter in the first eight seconds of someone's gushing explanation of something or other. He turned it off.

The breakfast room was almost full, but no sign of his client. Making a croissant and coffee last an hour till the room was empty he went to the foyer and asked the concierge whether he'd seen Lazen. He hadn't. Realising neither he nor Lazen knew each other's mobile number, he went to the nearest metro and, feeling a little like a minor victim of chance, shut his eyes in front of a metro map and touched the point of his pen on it. As he travelled to Saint-Michel he felt a little disappointed that it was so near. From there he could see the Ile de la Cite and its cathedral again and made his way vaguely towards it. He turned into a street and stood outside Shakespeare and Company, a bookshop in which he'd been asked a few years ago by a magazine editor to read some of his poetry. He'd declined the offer. The exterior was seductive, but the interior, with its floor-to-ceiling books and piles of them covering nearly every available space, had, to James, a too jumbled, cloying, self conscious aesthetic. He preferred its smaller, ordinary counterparts in Portobello Road or Hackney.

As he walked on, he heard a man's voice speak his name. He turned towards him not quite recognising him for a moment then remembered him as a student friend he'd first met on a counselling course some years before - leaving it because of the superficiality of its cognitive therapy bias. They shook hands, his acquaintance asking him what he was doing in the city.

'A kind of holiday.'

'Que le monde est petit. I'm here for a psychotherapist conference. It's just finished.'

'Good job your French is fluent, eh?'

'Quite.' He looked at his watch. 'I'm travelling back this

CHAPTER TWO

evening, but promised myself I'd see an indigenous film while here without the subtitles, though this version does have them for some reason, so you can come with me if you wish, we can catch up while we walk. You like French films, anyway. I remember.'

He did. It was the sound, the mystique of the language whatever was being said, that seduced him - a similar reason for enjoying operatic songs in Italian and not English, wary that the latter may reveal a libretto where someone is asked in Pavorotti-like tones whether they'd like a cup of tea or what they thought of the weather. It was nearby, thus not allowing them much time to talk, mostly the ex-student doing so; about the old days, what he was doing now and the conference.

It was a long film shot almost entirely in a Paris flat occupied by an elderly couple, the woman having Alzheimer's. It was an interesting movie, but towards the end James' attention drifted to the usherettes he'd seen quietly moving about the foyer between showings. He wondered if they'd always worked in this cinema or in different places. Maybe some had served in a churchlike Athens Odeon, an act of observance and Greek dubbing, others in Sao Paulo's Una Banco pimping ice cream while waiters touted margaritas, a Tangier picture palace, perhaps, where the audience shouted 'Look behind you!' to the hero or comforted refugees in a shell-pocked art house in Beirut. Maybe one had watched contraband movies in an Art Deco theatre amongst Havana palms, another fought off the manager of the Roxy in Taiwan. They'd heard the roar of light hit the screen, the ping of a bra strap from the back row, watched a lit match passed like an Olympic flame across red velour seats. Torch beams gliding over carpets they were ciphers guiding audiences into the city, its mansions, bedrooms and bars. He became aware of one next to his aisle seat leaning back on the curtained wall, raised knee flicking off a shoe, unlit torch idly hanging; the world at 24 frames a second in her eyes.

As they left the cinema James' colleague asked him what he'd meant earlier by being in the city on a 'sort of holiday.'

'I'm attending a client, well, I'm supposed to be treating him, but he's... elusive, it's difficult to get the feel of him, though I did only meet him two days ago.'

'Why here?'

'He happens to be English and can afford me being shipped over. I was given him by Morgan and Bayer. Lazen's his name, though I shouldn't be telling you that.'

His listener looked surprised. 'I think I've heard of him. Apparently he's been to a couple of other practices also.' He turned to James as they walked. 'Not our sort, more Bond Street and Mayfair. Gossip says he's been going around attempting to bribe practitioners, as it were, flinging money at them, something like that. The magic wand syndrome, a sign of desperation.'

'If there's desperation, isn't that our business?'

'Sure, but these people haven't taken him on. Probably it's all been exaggerated, anyway. Wish you luck with him. Must go, James, we should have a meal or something when you return.'

He crossed the road, gave a quick look back and walked towards a metro entrance, its period lighting silhouetting him in the dusk.

James went late to the breakfast room the following morning. Lazen was there alone, looking more like a Fellini star than ever in a linen shirt, pale blue single-breasted jacket, dark glasses and loafers. James sat opposite him

'Before we begin, I'd like your phone number. Boring, I know, but useful.'

'No need, I have yours, got it from Morgan.'

James was about to ask him if he wanted more control over him than he already had, but desisted.

'What did you think of ... how can I put it, the - '

'Performance? You were good, so was she, though I understood little. But, as skilful as you seemed to be and as intriguing as it was, the obvious question is, why?'

Ignoring this, Lazen asked him to come that evening to Le Diplomat in Monmartre. 'The same time if you would. It'll be a little different.'

James nodded acceptance, saying under his breath, 'Yes, Mister Lazen, certainly Mister Lazen.'

It was very Montmartre: a triangular bar at the convergence of two downhill roads, a red awning, potted plants on the pavements,

CHAPTER TWO

imitation *fin de ciecle* gaslights and velvet covered bar stools. He was a little late, his quick look around the area taking longer than he thought.

Sitting at a rear table away from the main throng, she was wearing a black pencil-slim skirt and tailored jacket, making the theory that, because black absorbs light women using it to look slimmer actually appear bulkier, seem utterly erroneous. Again she had a book with her, James suspecting it was a theatrical device.

After ten minutes or so, a time he spent mostly looking at the ancient Pernod posters and at her being apparently engrossed in her reading, Lazen walked in and also went through to the rear. He looked rather too smart; well cut jacket, crisp shirt, even a tie - reminding James of the overdressed, suit-wearing manual worker on a rare visit to a west end play. He didn't look at James, but the latter guessed he'd been seen.

There was a vacant seat about eight metres from the girl. James took his drink and went across to it. As he asked a wandering waiter for some water Lazen got up and sat down at the next table to her. He bent forward and in a flat, London accent, said,

'Excuse me, d'you live 'round here often?' He laughed. 'It's okay, you just make me nervous, that's all.'

She looked up, frowned a little and asked why.

'Well, you're very attractive.'

'Thank you,' she said expressionlessly, looking down at her book again.

'Er, you don't know me, but I'm Mister right.'

'You are?' she asked, turning a page.

'Shall we talk about the weather then as if we was in England?'

'Why?'

'Obviously 'cos I want to talk to you.'

She looked up. 'So you wish to say something of consequence then?'

'That's better, darlin', you smiled.'

'I don't like the 'darling'

'I knew you was English, dunno why.'

'Because I don't look French?'

'This bloke goes into a pub with a giraffe. He orders drinks for both of 'em, and then more and more. After a while the giraffe starts slipping to the floor, legs splayed. Barman says, "'ere, you can't leave that lyin' there.' 'It's not a lion,' says the geezer, 'it's a giraffe."

She laughed, a pealing sound, a long flash of white teeth,

'This bloke sees a dog in a pet shop window with a sticker on it saying 'Ten quid.' He goes in and the dog starts talking to him about his life; how many pups he's sired, kennels he's lived in, jobs he's had and working as a government spy. The astounded bloke says to the owner, 'It can talk. How comes it's only a tenner?' 'cos he's a fuckin' liar,' he says, 'he never was a spy."

She laughed even more, green eyes looking at Lazen appreciatively. James, trying not to make it too obvious that he was watching them, was engrossed, not sure whether she was playing a role or just being herself. Lazen was almost spivish; east end and likeable, immersed in his part, that rather deadened self James guessed was at his core now veneered with gloss. It was spontaneous between them, maybe they'd acted this one before, but James felt that they were good enough for the implicit premise - seemingly a bit of a Jack the lad trying to pick up a sophisticated woman - to be all they needed.

Lazen was consistently amusing her, there were no more straight jokes, they fed off each other as she talked to him more and began telling him about herself, he genuinely seeming to care. James couldn't hear a great deal of the rest because the music volume had been turned up and more people had come in. He tried to mentally formulate a script from what they'd said, were saying; wishing he knew more formal shorthand other than the crude one he used in his practice.

A short while after they left, Lazen, again courteously letting her lead and repeating his knowing and rather annoying wink, James did, too. He could see them further down the hill heading towards a metro entrance. He began following them without thinking why. He kept at some distance, but could see how animated they were, he with his arm around her waist. They went into the station, as did James, who stood at the near end of the platform watching them. He wasn't sure why he was there. Lazen kissed her quickly on the cheek as a train came in then left as she boarded it. James stood there feeling as if he were in a Michael Mann film: the subdued primary colours, he in foreground silhouette, the grainy, grey blues of the mid distance, a train clacking away and, as it turned a bend, its red tail lights hovering for a second above his shoulder. He returned to the hotel on his own.

The implicit ritual was observed again the next morning, both arriving on this occasion at the same time. Lazen quietly and earnestly ate his breakfast and, when noting James had finished his, got up to leave, beckoning him to join him.

As they walked, Lazen looked at him with interest. 'You like architecture, don't you. I must admit I feel more at home in the built environment than in the country. As you guessed, I don't walk enough, but when I do I tend to look up, like yourself, I've noticed you. They're the good bits, aren't they; you know, the odd castellation on top of an Edwardian hotel, a pediment above Victorian keystones or the set-back top of a thirties block. I guess I move slowly then and it seems to annoy people sometimes. I'll walk steadily, even-paced, disturbing no-one, yet people stride across me, forcing me to halt and not acknowledging it. Sometimes I'll flick out my foot and catch their heel. They'll stumble and glare at me. I just shrug, raise my eyebrows, feign apology and smile.'

He was quiet again, then, 'I was once walking along a side road off Boulevard Saint-Denis when I saw outside a church the trappings of an accident. There was an ambulance, a cordon, gendarmerie siphoning traffic, a stretcher, oxygen mask, a broken shoe on the road. I saw it all through a rush of paramedics and people leaning on barriers.' He turned to James. 'Perhaps part of them wanting to watch death, eh? Then this woman ran in front of me, laughing and knocking my arm. She tripped as my foot snaked out and I caught for an instance the black eyes, blind to me, on the road, but she wasn't laughing, she was wailing, *'Non, non, non'* as a gendarme ran to her and guided her to a car, the top of her head hitting the rim of the door arch as he pushed her in. I can see her dreadful stare now, trying to see the figure in the street under the blanket. I turned my back and glanced up at an alabaster Jesus above the church entrance and riveted my eyes on the gash of colour on its lips. It was like the woman's mouth; so red.'

James let him internally recap the incident for a while then asked if he saw those people who interrupted his progress as doing it purposely.

'It felt personal.'

'You don't watch yourself watching you at those moments, do you, you're feeling them, however quasi-paranoid it may be. Courtesy, manners are largely a function of space and numbers; so many people in a city, so little space.'

Lazen wasn't listening. 'That woman,' he said quietly, 'that poor woman.'

'How guilty did you feel?'

'What, on a scale from one to ten?'

James repeated his question; there was no answer. 'Where's it from do you think, where, when do we first learn guilt?' It's probably when, as babies, other than shitting ourselves, we bite mum's nipple and she pushes us away. Guilt and rejection; not a nice combination. The theory is ruined a bit, though, because there are some cultures where the woman doesn't push the child away, thus encouraging it to continue.'

'And there'll be psychological reasons for that too, no doubt,' said Lazen in a rather bored manner. 'Maybe the mother feels more wanted if the child's biting her. Anyway, what did you think of yesterday's one then?' He asked it with an almost childlike smile and metaphorically rubbing his hands.

'It was enjoyable, but you could play these scenes privately, could you not; in a hotel room or at home. '

'Not as exciting as in a real locale in front of people. Even if they don't hear us they can see us.'

'What prompted you to first approach Morgan and Bayer?'

Another silence.

'Enough is enough.' James could feel his good intentions leave him like an exorcised spirit. 'You need to talk to me, preferably now. I'm guessing a childhood trauma, Mister Lazen.'

His listener looked instantly both frightened and angry.

'Okay, tomorrow. I promise, really.' He took a rather

CHAPTER TWO

strangulated breath. 'Why don't you go off somewhere, do something you want, on me. The Folies Bergère, perhaps, I believe it's still extant.'

James wasn't in a mood for the still nudes, old photos of which lay in a black velvet covered programme of years before in his bedside chest at home.

'Enjoy your day.' said Lazen and tuned back in the direction of the hotel.

His day wasn't enjoyed, though there was some sort of escapist satisfaction in walking through the rain, the colours of streets and buildings washed away as a steady drizzle dropped flimsy layers of cool wind and a fine, blurred greyness around people hurrying along in their momentary self-sufficient worlds.

Next morning he awoke aware that this was his fourth one waking in a room three doors away from his client and determined that he was going to pierce more of the man's armour. He went downstairs early, ate with some of the other residents and as he finished his meal, Lazen bent over his shoulder and quietly invited him to his room.

James followed him in, not noticing the room's contents, just a tired, anxious looking Lazen beckoning him to sit as he rested on the edge of an unmade bed. As James sank into an armchair he gazed at him with a long-practiced expression of subtle encouragement.

The room's tenant looked at him almost shyly. 'I had this dream last night; I suppose they're important, really.'

'Depends whether you see the subconscious as benign, helping the self to confront, to unravel, repair.'

He looked away towards the window. 'It started off with chimneys, the London ones, those lip-potted, largely unused clay cylinders that, as a Londoner, have surrounded me most of my life. But it wasn't those or the architectural details of the houses that seemed important; it was the images of me as a child that I was swamped by. I was running along this un-adopted road at the edge of a wood I used to play in, past the tree leaning against the bowed wall, the gaps in the spear-tipped railings, the trimmed hedges, and hurtling across the heath away from my mother's heavy hands.' He looked at his listener. 'She used to hit me sometimes, but only because she couldn't articulate what she felt, was frightened, full of religious ideas of wickedness. I remember telling a boy what spunk meant and his mother coming to our house and telling my mother about it, I could hear them. She was so angry. I hid behind a privet in Alma Terrace, Then, in the dream, I was in my father's garden shed with its cobwebs and rusty mower and as I woke it triggered more real memories and I was crouched in the branches above the shed, then laying face deep in the grass in the park then bunking in the Gaumont to see 'The Bowery Boys,' and just ordinary things you do as a boy.'

'What did the dreams mean to you?'

'Don't know.'

'This doesn't sound like a rich kid's childhood.'

'No, it wasn't, we lived in south London until dad won some money from somewhere then made more from shares and things. I don't know the details. It doesn't matter.'

'What *does* matter?'

He turned his head towards James and leant forward. 'Look, here's my theory. The more self there is, and I don't mean selfish or what's called ego, but just being a… person. The more of that there is, the more feeling, then the less intellect, less awareness, perception; a pure intellect, if you like, with no emotions to cloud it.'

'You're positing a limited psychic space then?'

'There should be an absolute god, cosmic, all knowing, a god that fills everything with… People are merely creatures, just - '

'What is it that this god should know? It should know *you* shouldn't it, recognise you, acknowledge you. And who is a child's first god? Father, Mister Lazen, father.'

'Yes,' said Lazen, ignoring what had just been said and bending eagerly towards James. 'I *am* my intellect, the - '

James raised his voice. 'You don't want to face yourself, *feel* yourself, do you. You are perennially detached; perhaps see consciousness as a thing, *of* itself, especially your own, not as a being *for* itself. Let yours be for itself. You have the right to be a self.'

Lazen was looking down, hunched and still. James thought of

CHAPTER TWO

Sartre and the idea that consciousness alone was pure, transcendental in the sense of it being impersonal and that it must divest itself of empirical self-experience to arrive at that 'unnatural, inhuman absolute ego.' But James knew that Lazen's problems were more than this; he desired this absolute, transcendent, escapist fantasy because of his fear of, his terror to face ... James didn't know.

Lazen got up from the bed, walked away from him and stood with his back against a wall. 'Look, I've told nobody this, but I caught him with a woman, at home, in their bedroom.' His voice rose. 'My *mother's* bedroom.' He looked down, there was a long silemce. 'It was awful.' The last words were so indistinct James could barely understand them. He was quiet again for minutes, face expressionless.

'Perhaps there were things between your parents,' James began gently, 'that if you knew now - '

'I'd forgive him?' Lazen shouted. 'I was ten, fucking *ten.*'

He walked towards the window and back again.

'Do you want to tell me what you saw?

'It was his penis, he was sitting down with his legs open, dark hair all around it; she was lying on her front, naked on the bed. I don't know who she was. It was horrid. His face, that bland, satisfied face.' He sat on his bed again. 'I try to understand, to logically comprehend, but I can't, and I don't want to.' He punched the edge of the mattress, the force propelling him forwards. He stood. 'I got my money from his will. I have a brother who got hardly anything; I send him some of course. It was my implicit reward for not telling my mother.' He looked quickly at James. 'I feel tired now; I want to run away again. I can't keep here with you.' He went towards the door.

'If you were in my study and you'd booked yourself in for a fifty minute session you'd stay, wouldn't you?'

'No, I would have to leave.' He opened the door and glanced back. 'Thanks, sorry about the swearing. Let yourself out.' He closed the door quietly behind him.

James sat on the bed where his client had been, thinking of how lonely he must be. How could he have a real relationship with anyone based on just intellect, abstractions; 'Where is thought in the world?' Yes, a few moments here, some hours there with a friend or two, James suspecting he had few, but nothing lasting and not with a woman. For James, women had a different intellectualism; their primary concern was in just being and, to a man like Lazen, their emotional kernel was too solid. He would want the intellectual sharing of all his abilities with the one woman. It would be a kind of possessive acknowledgement, an intellectual and all-embracing recognition. It was impossible. He was, James suspected, an emotional orphan, the child in him seeking a parent. And how aware was he of what he was striving for? He couldn't, James guessed, compartmentalise his needs, no 'horses for courses,' this person to satisfy that one, that person another.

He left Lazen's room and the hotel and spent a large part of the day riding on the metro and thinking of him. As makeshift and staccato as the relationship was, he, at least for now, was seeing him every day and perhaps this was better than the weekly visits of his usual patients - when he had them. He shook himself free of him and went to the Eiffel Tower. It had begun raining again so he didn't bother with its observation platform and misty views of the city, but stood underneath it and admired its *fin de seicle* engineering. He took shelter for a while under a nearby café's inevitable awning and, looking in and seeing some workmen consuming large meals accompanied by bottles of wine, guessed it was a French equivalent of a greasy spoon. The perverse joy of the one he occasionally used at home was contained in its atmosphere of speckled lino, fly spattered blinds, sunlight filtering through smeared windows to hit a cloud of steam, and the eternal war between bleach and grease. It was almost like a day care centre for window cleaners, artists and escapees from rehabilitation centres.

Pulling his jacket above his head he half ran to a bus shelter where he hoped to find a bus to take him either to the nearest station or the hotel. There were two youths and a woman with a headscarf standing in it. She glanced at him. He recognised her instantly. She looked away, removed the clinging scarf and looked back again, her eyes narrowed.

'Excuse me, but I'm wondering if you're a friend of a friend.

CHAPTER TWO

Sorry, but I thought I saw you with him on Pont Saint-Michel the other day. I may have been mistaken, if so I apologise.' She hesitated. 'Was it you? He said you were a friend, though it could have been acquaintance, I don't remember. You were in the same hotel as he. Am I right?'

Even with her wet hair drooping down the sides of her face she had a casual self-possessiveness, a strength he hadn't quite noticed before. He wasn't sure how to respond.

'Er, *'Que le monde est petit.'*

'It *was* you, then. You speak French?'

'No, but I've had that phrase said to me twice since I've been here so I thought I'd say it, too'

She was smiling at him, still with slightly enquiring eyes. At least, thought James, I now have an official title in Lazen's social millieu.

'Of all the bus stops in all the world.'

She laughed. 'How long have you known him?

'A week or so, we have common colleagues in London. You're not a native either, are you.'

'Non,' she said as the lights came on in the shelter.

She briefly turned to see if she could glimpse a bus coming through the rain. She dropped a glove from the pair she was holding. Before he could move she'd bent down and retrieved it. It was the way she did it, one foot turned outward for a second that prompted his question.

'The way you moved then, it was like a ballet dancer.'

'Yes, I trained in ballet for years, but as you can see, I grew rather too tall. I wouldn't have quite the figure for it now, anyway.' She said it matter-of-factly, without a trace of visible regret and asked him what he did.

'I, er, lecture here and there. And you?'

'Oh. I act a bit here and there.'

'Do you get much work in Paris?'

'Not much; bit parts, a little dancing. I speak enough of the native tongue to get a few speaking roles.

'What's the biggest part you've had?'

'I played Simone de Beauvoir, in English of course, at a fringe theatre in London. It was strange to play a role without make-up,

I enjoyed it.'

They then asked in unison where each other lived. She told him she rented a flat in Bastille. Through the rain they heard a slowing bus. It was the woman's bus, not his. The youths jumped on before her.

'Strangers in the night, eh?' He had to raise his voice for her to hear. He hoped she hadn't. She turned towards him, the shape of her mouth suggesting a 'nice to meet you,' before she walked down the length of the bus and sat. Watching it splash away towards a clouded sunset he felt like a cliché hanging in the air.

He went to bed thinking that he now knew more about Lazen and at least he'd met the girl. It was he latter that prevented sleep coming quickly. He could so easily have got on her bus.

As he arrived late again in the breakfast room, Lazen pushed a chair back for him. He began speaking as soon as James was seated.

'I was thinking that we could have a ritual; you and I sitting down together at the end of a day and talking, then I realised I couldn't stick to it.'

'I'll get a tea and perhaps we can go to your room again. You can tell me more, anything that comes to mind, just things.'

'Let's talk here, there's nobody near us.' He removed the napkin that was tucked into his collar and sat back in his chair. 'Well, my mother was in a workhouse when she was four; one of a brood of six growing up in a world where the saying that all a woman needed to keep her happy was a 'pair of thick lips to kiss and a pair of thick boots to kick 'er' was a covert belief. There wasn't much joy in her life except for her friends' visits when my father was absent and her laughter when I or my brother would tell her outrageous jokes. In her later years, paper thin skin sucked tight into her temples and sunken eyes, she got angina, and she'd step and sway like a child learning to waltz as her arteries clipped blood from her brain. It was like a cryptic dance and she'd suddenly sit, as did my father, his back to her in the other half of the through lounge. He'd look puzzled that she wasn't in the kitchen and he'd salivate for food around shrunken gums thinking he may have to hold her upright again to cook his meal while her

CHAPTER TWO

slippers tapped this tottering staccato. I wasn't allowed to help. She could have had all the help she needed, but he didn't like spending money.'

'He used to claw his hands under her fleshless arms, shuffle her to the hall and drop her in the stair lift. Button pressed he'd climb wide-legged after her and lift her onto the bed. When he'd come down I'd go up and put pillows under her head. It was as if the house she'd befriended had turned enemy and I'd watch the tears spread through the lines on her cheek. I could hear him downstairs making his tea.' He looked out of a window again, watching passers-by, James momentarily doing the same.

'You know, when I hear someone use a word I haven't heard before or make an observation I've missed or discuss a concept that's new to me I feel a sense of relief and it's because there's intelligence there, so, however briefly, I don't feel so much on my own then.'

'Your alienation temporarily disappears.'

'Yes. I'm glad you understand that, though it doesn't really help.'

'What would? What earthly sort of recognition?'

There was no answer. James asked him his degree subject. That flash of annoyance again. 'I haven't one. But I've read a lot, philosophy, the metaphysicians, positivism. Have you read any of the Vienna Circle, it's -

'A degree would give you recognition of sorts though I feel your intelligence is floating above that.'

"Floating above'? You're trying to turn me into my own transcendental god.'

'But then you'd need it legitimated by an external one. You know this. Do you feel any different after telling me about your father?'

Lazen looked around him tensely and didn't answer.

'How long have you been escaping into your dramaturgicals or, rather, the particular form you enact in the bars?' Always with the same girl?'

His client became animated. 'No, different girls.'

'Do they do it willingly or does money buy their enthusiasm?'

'Sometimes, but it's such - '

'Fun, escape, denial? Do it in London, too?'

'All over, really. I don't have a private jet or yacht, I don't need possessions, conspicuous consumption's not for me, but this is something so much better, it's... You go into a bar in, say, Athens, and maybe you've never been to that city before, and we make our way separately to it and - '

'We?'

'Girls, women I may meet somewhere. But, sometimes, even if people don't understand what we're saying, that's if they can hear us, it may infringe local values or laws. Like in Baghdad once, we played a pre-arranged one, another me picking up a woman scenario. The locals got the drift and though, of course, there were no obscenities, you could feel the hostility building. The manager told us to leave.' His eyes were gleaming. 'Some girls are better than others at it, of course, I don't like it when they can't act.' He glanced quickly at his listener, 'I still pay them in one form or another, but it's great when they get it right, it's so... real.'

'But not quite as real as if it *were* real.'

Lazen shifted uneasily in his chair.

'Actors do what you're doing, in a professional capacity of course, and it's well known that a lot of them are shy, they hide behind their roles, but, acting a self as you do is attempting to fill a vast void.'

His voice rose defensively as if he were being attacked. 'I'm not harming anyone Mister Kent.'

'I could say, 'except yourself,' but part of you knows this as it's also aware that you can't get outside of society which a bit of you may be trying to do. Society is a prison and we are willing captives. We internalize everything, it becomes a large part of us, all is arranged; this hotel, shaking hands, stopping at traffic lights, all is institutionalised within a political and economic system. It's like attempting to get outside of language; that statement itself being part of language. Similar, perhaps, to your infinite, detached observing.'

A female concierge entered to tell them that staff would be coming shortly to clean the room. They left, James tentatively turning toward the stairs in case Lazen wanted him to go to his

CHAPTER TWO

room again, but as he was walking towards the exit it seemed obvious that he didn't.

'I need to go now, be on my own,' He momentarily lifted his hand and went through the revolving doors, leaving James to watch them turn slowly to a halt.

CHAPTER THREE

He was getting used to his client running away, as he had over the years, accepted others doing so and for far longer than Lazen. He decided to look for some more Art Deco and went to Rue Mallet-Stevens' cubist houses and to Moreau's rather disappointing, over formal classical garden. He then charmed his way into the extravagant, myth-like Rex cinema where he sat in its grand hall surrounded by wall reliefs depicting the French Riviera under a ceiling of star-studied sky. Shaking himself from his pleasure palace induced stupor he went out into a windy, leaf scattered afternoon. He took his time lunching and, not being in a mood for any 'grand' Paris, ambled around a few side streets, unable to resist purchasing a photo of a half built Eiffel Tower, looked around a small, tucked-away overgrown graveyard and was about to return to his room and continue with a book on Heidegger he'd brought with him when he spotted a bus to Bastille and stepped aboard it. As it moved away he could see in the distance the Rex tower lit as if it stood atop Heaven.

Not really interested in the July Monument, he made for the cobbled side streets and their small shops and bars, imagining Lautrec drinking with a new model in the latter's rich red interiors before taking her to Cormon's studio. He ate in one of the postcard and poster covered cafes before more wanderings through the brightly lit alleys. As he turned into one he pulled back quickly to avoid a woman hurrying along the cobbles with a large bag. He knew who it was. She stopped.

'It's you again.'

'I'm not stalking you, honestly.'

She smiled. 'I'd like to talk, but...' She began to walk quickly away.

'Anywhere nice?' He almost shouted it.

She looked back. 'It's a show.'

'Bit part?'

'Small part. Coming?' She asked it as if it was a challenge.

He caught up with her, briefly feeling that he was increasingly following around the city people he'd just met. They walked quickly through the warren of narrow streets.

'Sorry about this, but I can't be late.'

'That's okay, has it been running long?'

'A few days.'

They went into yet another alley, this one with a door over which hung a faded sign with *entrée des artistes* painted clumsily on it. She knocked on the door and turned to him.

'You can't come in this one; you have to go to the front.' She gave a pre-occupied wave as the door opened then hurried in.

He went around to the entrance, paid at the makeshift box office and absorbed the atmosphere for a few minutes over a coffee. It wasn't dissimilar to one he occasionally frequented under a railway arch in Southwark; bare brick walls, playbills of previous shows, a small bar and an audience quietly chatting. Through the curtained door the interior was larger than he expected with seats in a semicircle and some, with pseudo plebeian trendiness, set at the sides on metal scaffolding.

He sat towards the front of the fast-filling space, the darkened stage looking rather minimalist; just a few chairs and a slightly raised dais at the rear on which a few musical instruments lay. Six female silhouettes entered and sat on the chairs while male ones picked up the instruments. When the lights blazed on he instantly recognized the unmistakeable opening song from 'Cabaret' as a Joel Grey look-alike introduced the girls and the Sally Bowles character catwalked to the front.

For a second he forgot why he was here and then he saw her, slightly at the rear, straddling a chair before getting up and into that leg stretching, chair twirling choreography. It seemed she was playing Helga. Like the rest of the Kit Kat girls she was wearing suspendered black stockings beginning a few inches above the knees, a spangled top and a sailor's hat. She made intermittent appearances after this, spoke a few lines and did a little more dancing, but, other than the music and despite the clever deftness of an adapted script, the show, for James, couldn't really overcome its singularly sparse setting.

When it had finished he left and turned into the alley again, thinking of the flesh between the bottom of her tight black pants and the top of her stockings and wondering what her name was.

Because she was younger than him he also mused on whether she was familiar with the term, 'Stage door Johnny.' He waited under the sign for ten minutes before coming to the late conclusion that the cast may have left by the front. As he walked towards it the door behind him opened and the musicians came out followed by Helga and her bag.

'Hi, what did you think of it then?' she asked as she waved to the musicians moving off down the alley. He told her as they began walking the other way.

'He's a young director. I've mentioned the bricks, but he thinks it's trendy. I mean, how much would a few yards of shiny red curtain cost?'

'It certainly wasn't ballet was it, but you were good, very sexy. Hope you don't mind me saying that.'

She laughed. 'I was supposed to be.'

'But, over and above that; well for me, anyway.' He felt himself almost blush. He was regressing to a fourteen year old in front of her. He asked if she wanted to eat.

'There's a place over the road; I nearly said *rue* then.'

'How long have you been here?'

'About six months. An agency got me a part in a dance thing in Lyon. I was there a few weeks then a few more bit parts in theatres like the one you've just been in. Anyway, I'm learning the language.'

They sat in the café and ordered, she sitting upright, a high-necked jumper resting gracefully on her shoulders. She asked him how long he'd known Lazen. He was unprepared for it, though knew it was coming.

'A couple of weeks, I suppose. I told him I was coming here and, as he was too, suggested I stay in the same hotel.' He changed the subject. 'There's something about the colours of the food in French cafes, isn't there, so different from the heart attacks-on-a-plate English ones. Raymond Blanc thinks the English hate food and live in a very dark country where they go into revolting cafés and eat something disgusting to endorse their working class status. He blames it on Empire.'

'I don't know your name.'

'Nor me, yours. I guess it's not Helga.'

CHAPTER THREE

'It's Hannah.'
He told her his.
'Jimmy?'
'No.'
'Well, James, want to tell me about you?'
'I'd sooner you tell me about you, I know about me.'

'That's one way of getting out of it. Born and raised in true blue Buckinghamshire, dancing classes, in a London ballet company when I was twelve, then at seventeen, and increasingly looking down on male dancers' heads, it became pretty obvious I wasn't going to continue in ballet. Went to drama school, managed to get some parts, as said, and, of course, there's been the usual waitressing, etcetera. Oh, and one parent's a doctor, the other's a charities manager; solid middle class background. When's he coming with our food?' She gently tapped a knife on the side of a wine glass and smiled sweetly at a passing waiter.

James didn't usually like watching people eat even when eating himself. He enjoyed watching her. It was partly her old-fashioned, ergonomically maximised knife and fork correctness, her full lips and, mainly, because it was her. He knew he should attempt to get her to talk about his client; gaining a few behavioural clues here and there perhaps, but didn't want to, he wanted her to talk more about herself. She told him some amusing things that had happened when waitressing and, as their meal ended, decided she needed to go home and rest.

'Is it far?'
'Half a mile.'

He walked with her. Again, the narrow roads and alleyways, she refusing his offer to carry her bag and relating a few more entertaining restaurant staff incidences. They left the maze and turned into a road. She stopped.

'Well, this is it.' she said, gesturing to a small apartment block behind her. 'I'll see you again maybe.' She put the bag down, took a tissue from her pocket and said, 'Keep still.' and gently wiped a smudge of food from the corner of his mouth. She wished him a good night and went through the entrance towards the shadowy figure of a concierge.

Lazen wasn't at breakfast the next day. After he'd eaten, James checked whether he had any emails and found one from a current patient who he'd encouraged to contact him if he felt the need. It was his only message. After answering it he decided to walk aimlessly again. He passed that rather skinny St Paul's, the Pantheon, and had a look at an original Art Nouveau metro entrance before calling in at a place called 'Time For tea.' It had tea cosies, fifties pop music, floral table cloths matching the loo wallpaper, a photo of the young Queen and disappointingly crammed with elderly, mostly female English tourists whose 'oohs,' 'aahs' and 'so I saids' suggested they hadn't an idea in their bobbing, cackling heads.

He went out and walked quite a way before he tired and noticed he was in a familiar area of more alleyways. He wasn't quite sure where he was in relation to the previous evening, but came out of one of them at the other side of the apartment block where he'd left Hannah. He crossed the road to a café and ate his meal while occasionally looking out to watch the Frenchness of it all from a window seat. He was about to leave, this time keeping the receipt, when he saw her crossing the road towards him. She came in saying *'Bonjour'* to a woman behind the counter who asked if she wanted her usual. She nodded and turned towards the window table.

'What are you… ?'

He held his hands up. 'I'm just as surprised as you. I got here by accident, really. I was just walking around, though I did recognise the block,' he said, pointing to it. 'Did you know that the favourite word for the English is 'serendipity'? If you're going to stay here for a while it will be. Are you?'

'Yes, I have a kind of psychological ownership of this place, I'm often here.' She looked at him directly. 'You know, I think your subconscious drove you here in the hope of seeing me.' She laughed. 'You need an analyst.' Seating herself opposite him she glanced at his chair and said, 'That's my seat, the one I usually have, but don't get up, I forgive you. My favourite's 'vermillion.'

'It was Wilde's, too. Mine's 'sayanora.'

'We're playing the 'my favourites' game aren't we. What do you think of Karl?'

CHAPTER THREE

'Likeable, entertaining, I've hardly seen him since I've been here. I do at breakfast sometimes. He always seems to have plans; people and places to see.'

Her omelette was put on the table. She began to eat.

'What sort of things do you do with Karl. Does he come to your shows?'

'He hasn't yet.'

He watched her eating her meal. She wiped her mouth with a napkin. 'Well, what we do. It sounds crazy, but he likes it, I do to. It's difficult to explain, really.'

'Try.'

'We playact, One of us will go into a bar or somewhere, usually me, and he'll come in and act a part, maybe a Lothario of some sort, he has quite a range of accents, he's good. He mostly attempts to seduce me. I don't always know what he's going to be, neither does he, so we improvise. I do occasionally draw from characters I've played on stage, of course. He loves it, especially I think, when he knows people can hear us, believe us; he's the centre of attention, I suppose. He's not narcissistic, it's just good fun. We've been doing it for a while now. He pays for the drinks and, sometimes, food of course. I think he's pretty wealthy, though he's not, as I'm sure you know, flashy. He's a nice man, I like being with him, he's fun, creative.'

She drank her coffee, looked up and smiled. 'You can imagine what he was like when I told him I was an actress, can't you.'

'Where did you meet?'

'It was in a café next to a theatre during a short break between shows. I was wearing a nurse's uniform, I hadn't bothered to change. I was on my own. He was sitting there and came over and asked if I was a nurse. When I told him what I did his eyes lit up. 'Got time for a little scene now?' he asked, 'just a few minutes. Look, I'll be a surgeon, how's that? You start.' So I did. I couldn't imagine doing it outside of an audition, but I did. I said something that a theatre nurse, forgive the pun, would typically say and he became a surgeon, sounded like one, even looked like one. He was so convincing. I don't think he's ever been an actor though he certainly could be if he had the discipline. As fun as it was for a few minutes I don't think it was for the people at the next table, the subject matter wasn't exactly conducive to an enjoyable meal. You forget, when doing it how childlike it is.' She paused. 'What do you lecture in?'

'Sociology.' He knew enough about the subject to make his answer feel reasonably valid to himself.

'Tell me a little about it.'

'Well, it's partly about models of man, man's nature, often diametrically opposed in its theories; it's a perspective on the world, a particular way of looking at it, if you like. And yes, 'man' does subsume 'woman.' Let's leave it till another time. What I was about to ask was whether you and he were an item, as it were; though I don't like the term, I imagine a couple embracing in a train's closing doors on which there's a notice saying, 'Items stuck in the doors can be dangerous.'

'Why would you think that?'

'Well, it's not what you say about him, but the way you say it.'

'We're not, really. I am fond of him. I think, sometimes, that he's probably played these little scenes we do all over the place.'

'With different women?'

'I suppose so, I don't know, he doesn't encourage questions.'

'Doesn't that make you a little jealous?'

She shrugged disinterestedly. 'I wanted him to play Sartre to my Simone de Beauvoir once, but he wouldn't. We could have done it at the Cafe de Flore, too.'

'Apparently, most French people die of freak philosophy accidents.'

'Incidentally, I've been offered a small part in a film. They're shooting soon.' Her smile was full of quiet pride. He asked her where she would have to go for it.

'It's set mostly in Montparnasse I think.' He asked if he could come and watch. 'I don't know if you're allowed to, I'll enquire.' She looked at her watch. 'Hell, I'm going to be late. What is it about you that makes me late?'

She got up quickly, saw him glance at her feet as if her bag should be there. 'They've provided me with a locker at the theatre now.' As they went through the door she said, 'You're easy to talk to. I've decided you don't need a psychologist after all, you should have been one. I'll have to get a cab. They're usually at

CHAPTER THREE

the corner.'

They walked the few yards to the rank and got the first one in the queue.

'I'll pay; I'm the one who's made you late.'

They spoke little on the short journey. At its end, and just before she opened the door, she squeezed his hand. He watched her knock on the stage door and hurry in as it opened.

He wondered whether he should watch her perform again, but then pictured her astride a chair before moving into that leggy routine and, deciding that he didn't want his frustration magnified, thought he'd walk about for a while then wait for her at the stage door. He'd gone only a few paces before Lazen rang to ask if he fancied some supper at the hotel. There was a brief business-pleasure conflict before he dutifully and rather reluctantly joined his patient.

The menu, or that which could be deciphered over its embossed coat of arms, was classic French. While his client ordered the rich, strong smelling dishes, James ignored them and had the steak frite and brulée. His companion looked across at him with a slight sneer.

'Bland taste, eh?'

'On the contrary, it's sensitive. I don't like sauces. Almost by definition they're stronger tasting than the actual food, therefore the latter is reduced to a mere texture for the sauces. The bland taste belongs to those people who have a need for them. And while we're disagreeing, why didn't you tell me that you'd designated me as your friend? Obviously I'm not going to tell anyone what I am doing here, but you should have told me.'

'How do you know I've told people '

'I saw the girl accidentally in Bastille.'

The question was ignored. They finished their meal in silence after which Lazen suggested they again go to his room.

James looked briefly around it. 'How different is this to your parents' room? You shouldn't really have gone in there should you. I shouldn't have gone into my parent's bedroom either when I was a kid. I found a packet of contraceptives there. Fear and guilt, it can be a crushing mixture. Yours must have been so much worse, especially if there was something before that, perhaps a long time before. Was there?'

'I'm jealous of every child I see. I was at someone's house recently and they had young kids and they were laughing and joking with them, they had a relationship. With me it was so grim; the mealtimes, we weren't encouraged to talk. Sometimes I'd be playing with my brother and accidentally hurt him. I'd soothe his wailing and we'd laugh around again and then we'd hear mum's key in the lock and he'd start crying again and she'd wallop me.' He stopped for a while. 'When I was a teenager I told my dad I'd begun writing a play and timidly asked him if I could show it to him. He said, 'Best leave all that to those who understand that sort of thing, son.' So… dismissive, so nothing.'

'I know it's not really a consolation, but you do have an amount of money that - '

'Do you think that actually matters?'

'There must be a few compensations and you can, at least logically, understand that your father was a victim of his original social class and that he - '

'Made *me* a victim. Ever thought how frail the concept of necessity is? For example, although the sun rising every morning means that the psychological grounds of it necessarily rising tomorrow has strengthened a tiny bit, the grounds for believing it will necessarily do so haven't altered one iota.'

'I'd like you to stop it. You know exactly what you're doing.'

Lazen had been slowly pacing around the room since they'd entered it, but not looking at his listener.

'Look me in the eye, it's important.' He gave James the briefest glance.

'You can't, can you. You can't look your *father* in the eye. Your child can't look at him.'

'Shall we stop now, I'm genuinely tired.' He beckoned towards the door. James wished him goodnight and left the room.

Lying on his bed, James realised that his Parisian life had become almost ritualized: Lazen and the built environment's aesthetic, its boulevards, avenues, alleys, Lazen's room, the breakfast room and the usual abrupt endings of their verbal exchanges. He was getting almost used to it. But not of the exotic accident of Hannah.

CHAPTER THREE

As Lazen's note lying on the carpet behind James' door next morning informed him that he wouldn't be seeing him that day, he took a leisurely stroll along the Champs-Elysées. He wandered under its chestnut trees, by its extravagant fashion shops, a discreet Macdonalds and the quintessentially Parisian frontage of Guerlain's. He ate at a less expensive restaurant than he knew Lazen could afford and once more forced himself to keep the receipt - the action not only jarring established principles again, but making him feel financially inadequate. He crossed over and walked in the opposite direction to the way he'd come, seeing it almost as a different street; in London, occasionally recognising a road late because he had walked down it previously only the opposite way.

His phone rang. It was Hannah. 'I texted Karl and got your number from him. Was that okay?'

'Of course, I've now got yours.'

'I heard a little while ago that we're filming tomorrow.'

'I bet you like saying the 'we.''

'I do. I received the script, rather the bits that concern me, late; it was here when I got home last night. The scene, as said, is in Montparnasse and I've got to be there early. You mentioned you'd like to come.'

He wondered if Lazen minded her asking for his number and how he would feel about him breaking their unarranged routine. As he and Hannah discussed when and where to meet he felt guilty, as if breaching the terms of a contract. The feeling didn't last long. Lazen rang immediately afterwards and asked him to meet him later at a place in Belleville.

He had a few hours to spare until late afternoon and spent them on the Rue de Belleville, noticing how much more artistically literate the graffiti was than London's, then on past the double spire'd church to the market. He climbed a long, steep, cobbled road, at the top of which, turning to get a view of central Paris below, he felt almost as satisfied as he had climbing a hill in Snowdonia when younger and looking down through a layer of mist to the quilt like, hedgerow'd landscape of North Wales.

The address was a small *pension* with a café beneath some

upstairs rooms. In one of them were a table, chairs and Lazen. The proprietor bought their coffees up. His client began almost immediately.

'You know, I'm not only an intellect, there's some humour and creativity there too, but the rest is a kind of impoverishment. It's dulling and awful'

'I know. And I can't fill that impoverishment for you of course; you have to fill it with feelings, however painful. It needs to be filled with you, a living, breathing, real you. It will take time, a long time. You know this, at least intellectually. You'd like to fill this void partly with love, wouldn't you. *Can* you love?' The response was the almost inevitable silent gaze out of a window.

'Do you want to tell me some of the jobs you've had?'

'A bit of this and that. Helped a friend in a start-up company in the earlier days of the web, did some courses at an art college, but got fed up with having to read certain books, specific chunks of dead, recycled trees in the British Library. I have an eclectic mind, difficult to stay very long with one thing. You've guessed this.' He looked briefly at James, a little shyness in his expression. 'I think we could become friends, really, there's something about you I like, I think.'

James noticed, as he had before, that Lazen wasn't quite so articulate when talking of feelings involved in a relationship or potential one. He considered his answer carefully.

'We do, it seems, have common social backgrounds, despite the north-south divide of the Thames, but I can't afford to push much of it onto you; I certainly can't allow the projecting of my child on to yours, it will confuse him, they would get intermeshed. It would be harder then for me to help you unstitch your own child.'

'So, we can't ride off into the sunset together.'

'I'm supposed to be helping you. I have to stay at some distance.'

His client was silent.

'It's occurred to me that you want *me* to be your god. I can't be. I'm not a symbol of perfection, something which cannot be attained, I haven't an unassailable intellect, absolute judgement, I'm a fellow human. You need to know that because part of you

CHAPTER THREE

has, possibly, transferred itself to me. You must separate. The damaged part of you, the child, musn't try to see me like that.'

His listener raised a fist as if to bang it on the table then stopped himself.

'You're allowed to get annoyed with me; it's fine, but I can't be what you want. No one can.'

'D'you know, I increasingly think that everything in the world is a tautology, that one, too, of course; maths, definitions... '

For a brief moment James was aware that he wasn't really listening, he was thinking of Hannah. 'Tell me more of your father.'

Lazen looked down. 'I glanced in my wardrobe mirror recently, I was naked, and I saw a tall man with well shaped shoulders and... ' He began looking distressed. 'I saw my penis. I touched it, cupped it.' He mimicked the actions in miniature. 'And I let it go, quickly. I didn't want it; it seemed fleshy. big.' He looked at James. 'I don't want a slit, I want nothing there. It seems so... ugly, unnecessary.' He tried a grin. 'God had to be female, only a woman would create genitals *outside* the body.' He paused a while. 'I was in this café in Neuilly yesterday and went up to the roof garden. I sat on this ornate iron chair and looked at a large bunch of Victorian china roses on the table thrusting aggressively towards me like petal'd vaginas and hybrid penises. I wanted to pick up this wrench lying in a corner and smash the heads off, destroy chunks of my childhood. I knew that if I did I'd see thick, white, bleeding stems in my sleep for weeks to come and - sorry, you asked me to tell you about my father.'

'You just have, again. I know it can be frightening. I had the tip of a finger accidentally cut off as a child and it turned septic, I used to go to the hospital every few days for a month. One day I walked into the wrong room and there was a nurse treating a naked woman. That bush, that dark forest. It was alien, unknown and also something forbidden. It's not called a 'bit of the other' by chance. Yet, deep down, like other kids, I knew I would have to do something about it one day, knew I would have to go there, visit it. It's at the back of our minds constantly at that age, knowing you've got to do it. For you, of course it's so much worse. What about a girl friend?'

Lazen shifted uneasily on his chair. 'I want to - '

'Run away from me?'

His client looked around the sparse room with its brown patch of damp in a corner and heavy, half closed curtains, put his elbows on the table and slowly lowered his head into his hands.

James felt his sadness. 'I can only guess how difficult it is for you. I'm not being insensitive here, but while we're having, if you like, a session, I should be analysing the psychoanalytic process itself to try to recognise what I, the analyst, feels as well as what you the patient does. I could learn more about myself from this process, but there'll be feelings, things I don't wish to explore. You *have* to explore yours.'

'Not at this moment, though,' said Lazen, quickly standing. 'Remy's a surprisingly good cook, try his steaks. I have a tab, put yourself on it.'

'Do you want to see me tomorrow?'

Moving quickly down the stairs, Lazen was almost out of earshot.

It was the earliest he'd got out of bed and onto a train for some while, its crowded demography predominantly manual working and loud. He got out at Montparnasse-Bienvenue, walked along Avenue du Maine and turned into a smaller road at the end of which were two men placing a public phone box, its upper glass panel removed, onto the pavement outside a municipal building. At the bottom of its steps were a mike boom, two cameras and what James assumed was the film crew. One of the cameras was moved towards the phone box while the other, being squinted through by its operator, pointed to the other side of the street. Hannah was standing there looking across to the phone box as if about to run to it. A figure at the top of the steps lifted a megaphone and shouted, 'Action.' As he did so, James noticed a group of passers-by crowding together behind her, one of them pointing to her. Immediately guessing they would be in shot he shouted to the director, 'Excuse me.' and pointed to the gawping audience. He didn't, somewhat disappointingly, hear the director yell 'Cut,' but somebody went quickly across the road and shooed the group away. James looked across to her. She was smiling at

CHAPTER THREE

him and shaking her head.

The director told them to start again and she ran across the road, reminding James of when she'd left the taxi on Pont Saint Michel. A man had appeared in the call box and, upon reaching it, she said something loudly in French to him. He gestured impatiently to her to go away. She kicked the box in annoyance and strode off. Megaphone man then said what James roughly translated as, 'That's fine, that's it here for now,' and came down the steps. As the boom was taken from above the box the actor came out of it and smiled at Hannah as she walked to one of the crew, said something to him then came towards James. She was grinning.

'You sounded so English, so polite and modest, but you saved the day.'

'I heard an American once say that an Englishman instinctively admires anyone with no talent and who is modest about it.'

'I doubt whether you're talentless. I'll pick up my stuff and be with you, I'm in no more scenes today.'

'Carry your bag this time?'

'Okay.'

She walked up the steps, her long legs gracefully transporting her to the top where she picked her bag up from a pile of props and came down again. She gave it to him and they started walking.

'All is illusion, uh? A cloth of fantasy stitched together by a director. But I have to believe it of course, I'm in it.'

'As?'

'Sister of the hero, the guy in the phone box. I'm annoyed with him because his girl friend, who I'm supposed to be fond of, is being made miserable by him ringing his other girls. It's quite French.'

'Other scenes?'

'Yes, one tomorrow. Maybe you can take over this time and start directing it.' She laughed and, as the sun momentarily broke from a cloud, put her arm in his. They walked comfortably back along the Avenue and then took a step down the stairs of the metro entrance. They both stopped.

'Why are we going into this station?' she asked.

55

'No idea.'

'I've a few hours before I go on. Suggestions?'

'Show me bits of Paris you like, you know the city better than me.'

'Okay, let's go down again and cross the river.'

They emerged ten minutes later from a sunny Boulevard exit with two buskers, one with a tenor sax, the other a trumpet, playing traditional jazz. They stopped and listened for a while, dropped a couple of Euro into an upturned beret on the pavement and, with her pulling him along, halted outside a small, run down bakery nearby.

'Follow me.' she said. As she wemt inside, a large, round woman with rolled sleeves and apron stepped from behind the counter and, grinning broadly, gave Hannah a hug, looking at James as she did so with raised eyebrows. He was introduced to Madame Thomas and while she returned to her till they sat at a single table in a corner.

'It's a friendly nook, this place. I think she does it for something to do, but she bakes the best baguettes in Paris.'

While they ate they talked of the cities they'd been to; between them picking out the delis in Manhattan, Madrid's lit fountains, Glasgow's surprisingly grand squares, Barcelona's Ramblas and Prague's graffiti.

'I was once a statue in the Ramblas. It takes discipline, especially when some half pissed cretin of an Essex mangirl pushes her face into yours trying to make you move.'

'What were you?'

'A kind of Eliza Doolittle made of lead. There were some good ones: a marble Columbus. a copper cast GI who gave a smirking salute when tourists dropped some cents, a bronzed centurion who'd raise his spear and a man made from chalk with a scowl and a guitar. I used to spin a little rose and blow kisses.'

'I can imagine you after a hard day saying to your boyfriend, 'I'm tired, I've been on my feet all day.''

'There was no boyfriend, I went because I had some work there; it didn't last long. And you?'

'Working class lad made bad.'

'White man speak with forked tongue.'

CHAPTER THREE

'Okay. Decorator, sign writer, commercial artist, professional.'
'Is this a holiday romance?'
'Hope not, they tend not to last.'

He asked her to show him somewhere else and after she and the bakery lady had hugged again, followed her out. They went to the Marais, watched the kids on the fairground roundabout on Saint Antoine Street, had falafel in the Jewish area with a *'pas de vinaigrette'* insistence from James, and then her belated realisation that she had little time to spare for her evening show.

'It's your fault,' she said as they hurried down the steps of another metro.

He decided to stay and watch the show again. This time it was made moving by the inclusion of the falsetto voice of a young singer playing a fair haired Hitler Youth. James felt the back of his shoulders grow cold as he listened. He met her at the stage door.

'When I carry your bag I feel like a schoolboy carrying a satchel for the girl in his class he has a crush on.'

'Do you have a crush?'

'Yes.'

She grinned at him. 'I could have left it at the location, the crew would have taken it for me to the one we're filming at tomorrow. Are you coming again? Be my groupie?'

'If Karl doesn't want to see me.' He couldn't get used to using the forename. 'I hope he doesn't.'

They walked to her block where they had coffee in her jumbled, book strewn first floor living room before she suggested, as she had work the next day, that he leave. As she went towards the door he pulled her back and kissed her, feeling her teeth thinning her lip. She moved slowly away.

'I'll see you tomorrow. Goodnight.'

He walked most of the way back to the hotel before catching a bus, pondering on why he wasn't feeling some excitement, some joy, instead of feeling a little lost. Less than two weeks ago he'd been staring at another anaemic wash of colour on his last piece of cartridge paper wondering whether to bother with any more unsuccessful attempts at water colour landscapes and also how he might be able to encourage more patients to consult him. Now, here he was in this foreign city getting paid handsomely to sporadically tend to a man whose psyche James hadn't managed to get to grips with yet on any meaningful level and becoming intrigued by and attracted to a woman who was increasingly detracting him from his job. His professionalism felt like an old coat of paint being weathered away.

Lazen was removing the napkin tucked into his collar when James came down next morning. He stood. 'I'm aware that you're hungry, but I'm at Versailles today and have little time. Come to my room, if you would.'

Once there, James sat on a chair again while Lazen paced.

'My whole life, really, has been an escape from a primal scream, a kind of undercurrent to it which I haven't released yet.' He clenched a fist and hammered a thigh. 'How can I scream if the part of me that's doing the knowing is stronger than that which wants to scream?'

'Forgive the repetition, but you need to fill the space occupied by the little man on your shoulder, as you call him, observing, intellectualizing, and fill it with yourself, with you.'

'I know. I know. I make my loneliness unreal, too. I can feel myself doing it. I do it with everything; other voids, impoverishments… there's not even a response when I use my name.' He looked at James. 'You can say something like, 'What d'you think you're doing, James?' and you feel yourself, you feel James. I get nothing, there's no answer, I have no emotional reference. Nothing.' He sat on a chair and lowered his head. James felt there were tears coming.

'When he was old I had a go at my dad once. Did you hear that? That's the south London in me.' There was a bitter grin. 'I shouted at him, never done it before. I told him that I hated being with them when I was little because I never saw him touch my mother, not a squeeze of her shoulder, an affectionate arm around her waist, not even a kiss on the cheek.' He'd begun to cry. 'How can *I* fuckin' love?' He gripped his thick hair with both hands and stayed, elbows on his knees, motionless for minutes. James didn't interrupt him.

He stood suddenly. 'I'd like you to go now, I think. Thanks. I'll

CHAPTER THREE

see you.' He closed the door quickly as James left.

As he rode along he wasn't really aware of the tram's jade green and cream combination of his favourite Art Deco colours, nor the gutter cleansing water gurgling from the avenues' culverts. He was thinking of the patients he'd had and his searching behind their faces to see if he could find the desperate child. He knew it was there with Lazen, but couldn't quite emphasise with it. It was the man's physicality he couldn't empathetically get beyond: his height, the leonine head, broad face, his presence, it stopped him getting closer - though this was taboo territory, anyway, the only 'closer' allowed was to get nearer to the genesis of the man's problems. Perhaps he was jealous of him and, a sudden awareness, of him and Hannah. It felt like the thought of a sulky child. Again, how quickly his professionalism, that reification representing the rules and guidance of his role, dissipated.

The scene was set at the edge of a small park in Montsouris. When he arrived, the crew were there packing things away, reminding him how late he was. He asked a cameraman whether she'd gone. She had, a few minutes before. He went back to the tram terminal. She was standing outside. He felt disproportionately relieved.

'I guessed you'd travel by tram. Your mobile's off, I tried to get you.'

'Sorry. How did it go?'

'Another first take. Just a quick chat with the boss and my 'brother,' a little rehearsal and we did it. We argue, he pushes me, I fall awkwardly and break my arm, he stalks angrily off. Actually, I did fall awkwardly, it was my fault.' He felt an urge to protect her.

'Oh, I didn't tell you, Karl brought me a lovely present. He delivered it yesterday; the concierge gave it me this morning. And I've a matinee today, but we've still time to go by tram. That's if,' she said with mock uncertainty, 'you want to come back with me.'

James had momentarily forgotten, perhaps purposely, that she and Lazen had a history. They had done things together; he'd been there at only two of them. He tried not to think what the present may have been.

He let her do most of the talking on the way back. At the stage entrance she kissed him softly on his lips, 'It's Sunday tomorrow, so no show and Karl wants to see me. We're going to another bar somewhere I think. I'll ring you.' She disappeared into the theatre, not asking him if he would be waiting for her later.

In the hotel bar he had a rare late evening drink, trying not to picture them in another scenario, this time with Lazen dressed as a hussar complete with plumed hat and dress sword, she as a Spanish princess coquettishly fluttering a lace fan. He smiled at his pictorial hyperbole and went to his room wondering if he'd be invited to the performance.

The breakfast room was full next morning, making his client's absence more pronounced. He went to the Bois de Boulogne, walked partly around its lower lake and returned to the hotel at dusk. As he entered the foyer Hannah rang. She was upset. She had begun her and Lazen's little bit of ersatz drama when it had, apparently, turned into a real one.

'We'd just begun. He came over to me all smiles; he was, I think, an old world aristocrat. He charmingly introduced himself as *le Comte* somebody or other and then said that he couldn't continue. He just walked away. I thought he was going to walk straight through the closed door.' He could hear traffic in the background. 'I'm on my way home now. Perhaps I'll see you tomorrow.' She rang off.

Opening the door to his room he again saw a folded note lying behind it.

I saw you leaving Hanna's building. I was near the entrance when you came out.

There was nothing more. It was written in the same terse, but grandly scrolled style as the previous one. Perhaps he'd returned to see whether she was pleased with his present. He wondered whether Lazen had imagined him on her bed with legs apart, erect penis and instantly morphing into his unfaithful father and, to make it even worse, was with someone he wanted himself. James

CHAPTER THREE

called him. The tone rang endlessly.

He had little sleep and woke from it early. On impulse, he went to the counter and asked a concierge whether she'd seen Lazen.

'He has left, M'sieur, he booked out last evening, I don't know where he has gone. He's been here two or three times before and usually lets us know in advance when he's leaving, but not this time. I'm sorry.'

He tried, unsuccessfully, calling him again. A few minutes after breakfast and returning to his room there was a tap on the door. It was Hannah. She stepped in.

'So this is where you live. I'm concerned about him.'

He was pleased she'd come. He told her that Lazen had left, but was unsure whether to tell her why, apparently, he had done so. James felt he'd been fooled, perhaps had fooled himself; he'd had little idea how Lazen must have felt about her, though it could be that she'd suddenly represented to him something that had been taken away from him, like his childhood, his ego. If so, it had been taken away by the very person he had trusted to help him. He decided to tell her.

'A note? Why didn't he just tell you, say that he saw you?'

'Because he didn't want to face what he thought you and I were doing.'

'What was that?'

'It's pretty obvious isn't it? He wouldn't expect it of me.'

'Because you're his friend.'

'Because I'm supposed to be here to help him'

'To do what?'

'Get better.'

'He's ill? You're really a doctor?'

'No, he has emotional problems.'

'You're not just his friend, then.'

'I'm not even that, I've known him only a few days. I'm sorry if - '

'You *are* an analyst, aren't you. Why didn't you tell me? You said you were his friend.'

'No, he told you that. I couldn't tell you why I was here, it would have been disloyal. I took it as said that he hadn't told you'

'So, your only interest in him is as a psychologist?' Her voice was rising.

'There are things I like about him, he has - '

'Are you going to analyse me next, then? How many therapists does it take to change a light bulb? Only one, but it's got to want to change. Oedipus, schmeedipus, who cares as long as he loves his mother? You're not a lecturer either, are you.'

He knew he had to tell her something else or it would fester. 'I'll be honest, I've seen you both in bars doing your playacting, I was sitting near enough to see and hear a lot of it.'

'You were spying?'

'He wanted me to observe him, he asked me to be there. It sounds voyeuristic, but it wasn't. I should have told you, but if he'd asked me again since I've known you, I wouldn't have. I leant little anyway, except that he's quite talented.'

She was shouting now. 'You asked me what I did with him and you'd actually been *watching* us. How could you lie like that?

'I'm sorry, but if I'd told you I was an analyst it would have frightened you off; no show, no watching you film, walking around. I was attracted to you when I saw you cross the bridge from the taxi. I didn't recognise it at the time, but I - '

'Well, this isn't acting now, this is real.' She paused. 'Soon after I first met him he used to look at me as if he wanted me, though he never even hinted at it, and when he sometimes drove away from a bar I would go all Antony and Cleopatra and say to myself, 'Oh, lucky Audi to bear the weight of Karl.' She paused again. 'I think I told you that to hurt you.'

He knew he couldn't tell her that Lazen wouldn't make love to her anyway, or why; it would breach protocol, and even as he thought it, knew he was using the institutionalised principles of his craft to hide the glaring fact that he wanted to tell her, wanted her not to want him.

'I assume you've tried ringing him.'

'Of course.'

'A text?'

'That would be anathema to him, specious words.'

She leant against the door. 'This isn't getting us anywhere.'

He made an effort to be pragmatic. 'Any idea where he could

CHAPTER THREE

have gone? He doesn't have to be in Paris still.'

She thought hard. 'There is', she said slowly, 'a favourite hotel of his in Rome, he used to tell me why he liked it so much, I forget the reasons now.'

James asked her for its name. She remembered it. He got the number and called. There was no one by the name of Lazen on their books.

'He doesn't need to use his own name.' she said

'But if it's a favourite place he'd be known there.'

'He could have told them that he didn't want anyone to - I feel frightened for him.' She looked across the room at him. 'He's your patient, I understand you're not supposed to have an emotional relationship with him, but he's paying you, isn't he? I don't know whether you have a contract or something, but perhaps he's become dependant on you, he probably likes you.' She was silent for a while. 'Are you really sure that you're not defining him as mentally ill because he's different? People are given labels like that because they go against current values, like protesters or draft dodgers; you know this, you teach... but of course you don't.'

'I've said I'm sorry.

She was agitated now. 'Forget all this, he needs help, otherwise you wouldn't be here, and I don't know why I think he's gone to Rome, but I know that he has. He needs us.'

'Is there an 'us'?' He was surprised at his courage.

'Maybe.'

'What d'you want to do? Just go there? Can you afford to?'

'For a short while.'

'But, your show, the film.'

'There's an understudy, she's promising, reminds me of me when I was her age. She deserves a chance. And I don't think they need me for the film for another two weeks or so.'

She walked across to him and gently eased him to the bed. They sat on the edge of it

'Come. Come for me.' She rested her hand momentarily on the back of his then slowly slid it away. It felt like a long burn. For a second he didn't want her to care, to worry about Lzen, then, in instant atonement, said,

'Alright, we'll go together.'

She squeezed his arm and left the room. Just then his mobile rang. It was Morgan asking how he was getting on.

CHAPTER 4

As the aircraft rose from Charles de Gaulle and he looked across at the city he felt he was leaving a place that he hadn't really experienced. There were only a few bits of urban magic and spiritual excitement that remained inside him, other than Hanna. He was no wiser about the origins of his client's initial trauma, either. He looked at her, worried and quiet, on the seat beside him. She'd spoken little since meeting him in the foyer of her block three hours before, the situation remaining the same as they descended into Fiumicino Airport with aircraft gathered around its flat box central building like piglets around a sow.

They went through Arrivals to the bus stop for Central Termini with James asking himself why it seemed such an insurmountable problem for English airports to have their grey and beige carpets ripped up and replaced with marble. Before they boarded the bus he tried, again unsuccessfully, to call Lazen. He looked out at the evening street lamps moving by then at her profile. Despite the adverse circumstances, maybe he could find some pleasure in his visit to this city, remembering from his previous one little more than the Coliseum and the Tiber's algae.

The two star hotel where he'd booked single rooms for a night with an option to stay longer was sparse and clean and apparently not too far from the one where Lazen may or may not be staying. At the top of the second floor stairs she whispered a quick, 'Thanks for coming.' and went to her room away from his at the end of a corridor. He resisted the temptation to offer to carry her bag.

She knocked quietly on his door in the morning and they went downstairs to the breakfast room, James feeling for a second that he wouldn't have been surprised if Lazen was in there reading *La Repubblica*. She hadn't slept well, dreaming of standing on a shore watching a fast tide foaming in and not knowing whether to splash in and swim into the sea or stay where she was, mesmerised by the water scurrying over her feet. James, resisting pointing out the emotive symbolism, suggested that after breakfast they ask the concierge the way to Lazen's possible hotel.

The Hotel L'Angelique wasn't far from the Borghese Gardens. It was a sumptuous Art Deco one which elicited a wish, unusual for him, to want money; to be able to book a room, a suite of them, and to have a chauffer-driven Rolls or Mercedes waiting outside. On a more realistic level he would liked to have seen Lazen and talk to him about the building and whether he saw it as merely grand or were there the little things; a ziggurat newel post or a table lamp made of a silver female figure holding a bow that intrigued him. He wondered momentarily and not for the first time if he sometimes liked buildings more than people and, if so, why. As they neared the counter he cupped her elbow and guided her away to a sofa at the side of the foyer.

'We've kept this unspoken so far, I know, but what do we actually say to him if he is here or if and when we do find him? Seeing us together will be a confirmation for him that we've slept together.'

She looked at him without expression. 'What do you think his reaction will be?'

'I don't know, but he could feel that we were enemies come to taunt him.' He couldn't tell her that, at worst, he would see his father and mistress harassing him; the physical reality of their psychic stalking that had been present for virtually most of his life. He felt restless. 'Let's go for a walk, clear our heads.'

She started moving to the entrance while he looked around the foyer. He lost himself in its chevrons and vitrolite tiles for a while till he saw her outside frowning in at him through the entrance door. He hurried towards her.

It was a warm morning. She was wearing a white, broad sleeved blouse and dark skirt, reminding him of Loren in 'Two Women.' It mildly amused him that, when picturing her in Paris, she'd looked a little like Anouk Aimee. They walked to the lake, set in landscaped gardens supposedly in the English taste but with trees never seen outside of Kew, and admired the villa with the statues at the apex and base of its pediment, its columned Romanesque radiating across the water. Her interest waning quickly, she told him she wanted to go back, her look suggesting that they hadn't come for the sightseeing but to ease her anxiety about Lazen. They returned to the hotel and, already knowing the answer, asked the concierge whether he had the name down as a current or recent guest. There was a brief hesitation and, perhaps, a forced casualness about his, 'Not here. *Egli non e restare qui.*'

They went out and, spotting a caffé across the road, went in. While at the counter he could see her sitting frowning down at her table. He placed a latte in front of her and sat. 'Put lots of sugar in it, you'll feel better.'

She looked up. 'Did you believe him?'

'Not really. Do you still feel he's here?'

'Yes.'

'We could, I suppose, keep a watch. Take it in shifts like the cops do; a stake-out.'

'They'd be in a room opposite with food, drink and binoculars.'

'We've got all that except the binoculars.'

'I can't just sit here all day.'

'And evening and, perhaps, night.'

'What do we do then?'

He tried to think of something, as he should have done before leaving Paris; the obvious need for a plan. Feeling a little better after apple cake she began to suggest reluctantly that they somehow do as he suggested, having little alternative, when a man came over to their table He was a little younger than James, thin and wiry with a large, toothy smile.

'*Mi scusi,* I thought I saw you come in here.' His English had just a trace of Italian. 'I hope you don't mind, but I overheard your conversation with the concierge, I was on my way up to fix their wi-fi, it was a quick job, I saw you come in here while I was doing it. It concerns the man you were asking about. I know him, he's staying here; well, he was two mornings ago. I wondered why you were told he wasn't.'

James beckoned him to join them and asked how he knew Lazen.

'Politics mostly, though I did meet him a little while before that.'

This surprised James; he couldn't quite see Lazen as an overtly political being.

'I'm Luca, by he way.' He looked quickly at Hannah. 'Should I tell you this?' He laughed. 'It was in a taverna off Via Giuseppe, we were both on our own and possibly drunk. He didn't really seem the sort for a place like that, it's a bit run down, perhaps he was slumming, I think you say. We got sentimental and talked about friends and family and so forth and, for some reason, I asked him his surname and realised it was a familiar one, but couldn't recall where I'd heard it. Well, a couple of weeks ago in Livorno I visited my grandfather who I hadn't seen for a while and he started talking, as ever, about the old days when his father had helped form the Party, the PCd'I, Partito Comunista d' Itlalia in Livorno following a split with the Socialist Party in the twenties.' He gestured as if he should have explained before. 'I learnt my English from my mother; her brother was a diplomat n England. I should, I suppose, have got my politics from them also, but, as you may have guessed, it was from my grandfather, the politics of dissent. His father knew Gramsci and was with him in support of the Arditi del Popolo against the Fascists. Anyway, during one of his tales he mentioned the name Lazen and then, of course, I remembered that he'd talked of him before. He hadn't known a lot about him, mostly that he was English, a Marxist, and very tall. Incidentally, Karl joined the Party the last time he was here a few months ago. He came on a couple of demos with us. He is a good man; 'ardent' is the word, I think.'

'When I saw him a couple of days ago - I seem to be constantly in that building, there's always something wrong with their IT set up - he'd just arrived. I told him what my grandfather remembered. He was so surprised his jaw hung open. It was funny. It was his father's father who he'd met only once as a child. Apparently, his dad never spoke of him. He immediately asked for granddad's address; wanted to see him. I thought it would be good for both of them, so I gave it. He was quite excited and said he'd go to see him soon.' He got up. 'Now I need to go. Enjoy *Roma* and I hope you find your friend. *Ciao.*'

They thanked him and watched him cycle speedily away. James turned to her. 'You were right then. He is, or at least was here. Intuition, uh?'

CHAPTER FOUR

'It's a relief. I wonder if he went to this place, Livorno, and whether he's still there. Is he still paying you?'

He rang his bank; money had been transferred that morning. Perhaps Lazen had forgotten to cancel it, but it could be that the lost child in him was still hoping that James could, somehow, still help him. They silently finished their coffee, he feeling a little inert and indecisive and thinking of his own grandfather with his cropped grey hair, collarless shirt, braces and boots and who'd knocked his wife's front teeth out in drunken anger.

'He's back again.' she said, gesturing through the window.

Stepping off his bike and dropping it in the kerb, Luca walked quickly across the sidewalk and into the caffé again.

'I'm glad you're still here, thought you may have gone.' He quickly pulled up a chair. 'I've just seen Sara, she's a *cameriera*. Sorry,' he gave a suggestive chuckle, 'chambermaid. She said he stayed two nights ago and when he saw her yesterday morning gave her a large tip. She told him that wherever he was going to enjoy himself. 'North west.' he'd said. Maybe he went to see granddad, I don't know. She's serviced different rooms since so hasn't seen him. He pushed his chair back. 'This time I really am going.'

James asked for his mobile number. He gave it, his toothy grin again in evidence. Once more they watched him cycle away.

He turned to her. 'It doesn't seem quite so desperate now, does it? He's been here, probably visiting someone or something, maybe he'll return and - '

'I want to go there. Perhaps the old man can tell us something; what he's going to do, where he'll be, when.'

James, for a moment, had the feeling that she really wanted to go to Luca's grandfather's house simply because Lazen may have visited it and his presence was still there. He pushed it away from him. She wanted to go because she was fond of him, was worried about him. He thought of her Anthony's horse analogy and wondered where the Audi was now.

He rang Luca and they went back to the hotel to arrange to leave their luggage then caught a bus to Barberini metro. She looked up at the Trevi Fountain as they alighted.

'All these people, sightseers, pickpockets; not quite like

Fellini's take, is it. I've always wanted to see it, but not at the moment.'

He glanced at its Baroque grandness, the statues in its walls, its formality, classicism and granite hardness; take the water away and it looked rather menacing. They travelled by metro to Termini where they were only just in time to catch the Freccibianca train to Livorno.

He would have preferred a slower journey. In the sunlight he wanted to see details; of villas, cypresses, low hills, Van Gogh-like hay bales, terraced vineyards, not a blurred rush of fences, petal less sunflowers and telegraph poles. He wanted this journey to be leisurely, fascinating, an affirmation of he and Hannah being here. He wished to fill himself with the Italian sun, the light. He rested his arm on her shoulder. She gave a barely discernible smile and bent forward to look at the landscape. He spent the two and a quarter hours of the journey listening to her short, intermittent tales, at his request, of the parts she'd played on stage and, in between, looking out and thinking of the places in Tuscany he would have preferred to visit: Siena, Florence and its cathedral and, instead of just stopping at its station, Pisa.

They reached Livorno Central where he admired its tall windows, high pillars and the marble and stucco of the ticket office while she walked ahead. In the tree-lined avenue leading from the station they caught a bus to Via Borra then a stroll to Little Venice before quenching their thirst in a small bar. They had just begun to do so when there was the sound of a trumpet and drums outside. As the volume increased about sixty or so people moved by, erstwhile musicians at the rear and led by men holding a banner with the words, writ large in both Italian and English, 'The ruling class is made up of thieves and mafiosa and are destroying our country. We are better than this. Out Out Out.' The synchronised shouts of *'Fuori Fuori Fuori'* were as loud as the drums. As they passed, a smaller group appeared behind them carrying a banner with a different symbol on it, the words in Italian. Most of the bystanders were alternately cheering and booing each group.

'She shook her head. 'Why do these people, these factions, spit

CHAPTER FOUR

and claw at each other?'

'If you're going against any all-powerful, all pervasive entity like capitalism, then there'll be many different opinions about what would, should make up its opposition. Capitalism's been around for a long while, it's the current hegemony; we barely see it as political. It's interesting that any attacks on it; protests strikes, etcetera, are seen as political and somehow morally wrong as if that which is being attacked isn't. It's just there, seemingly natural; the best way, perhaps the only way there is.'

'Especially in Buckinghamshire?'

'What did people want after the recent recession, a revolution? No, more of the same, but better.'

She looked at him. 'I can't imagine Karl saying anything like that and I don't think you can either, but, if he has become politicized, you have more in common with him than you may think. Maybe you can, even as a... person, help him.' He knew she hadn't quite forgiven him for lying to her. 'Let's see the man now; you said he lived around here.'

They walked along the criss-crossing canals and their vapid water, but despite the bright afternoon sun there was a darkness, and not just the canals, the streets also. They were narrow, the buildings not high enough to block the light, but, somehow, the walls and the small, iron grilled windows, narrow pavements and cobbles were in shadow. Then, in a surreal moment - he'd forgotten that they were in a large port - he saw, through a gap between buildings and perfectly framed in a blue sea, a cruise ship, and knowing that the Cinque Terre villages weren't far to the north, wished, untypically, he was a cruise ship passenger so that he could step off at them: Riomaggiore, the terraces of Coriglia, Monterroso...

The address he'd been given by Luca was an old terra cotta painted house in an alley a little away from the canals. It had bright red flowers on the sills and in large pots at the side of a red door, possibly, thought James, purposely representative of the owner's political convictions. The polished brass knocker made a ringing thud and an elderly, lined face appeared as it opened. James introduced them both.

'I believe Luca told you we would be coming today.'

'Of course.' He bowed his head. *'Inserire,'*

The passage was short and narrow, the front room opening off it filled with a large sofa and armchair with prints and photos spread over the walls. He gestured for them to sit.

'You are friends of Edward's grandson, then?' It was more a statement than a question. 'I shall make tea.' His accent was heavy.

He limped into a kitchen at the back and returned with a tray and a large teapot, explaining that the latter had been bought for his father by Edward when he'd first got married. He poured then sat facing them.

'I believe you want to know about your friend. Do you know that he was here yesterday?'

'We guessed, hoped he had,' said Hannah, 'your grandson wasn't sure. We're bothered because he's been depressed lately and are rather concerned.'

'He wasn't when I saw him, I must say,' the old man said happily, 'He was interested in anything I could tell him of the old Party and, of course, his grandfather, especially when I told him what a committed Marxist my granddad said he was.'

He stood and gestured expansively to the mostly black and white photos and pointed to those of himself with a Zapata moustache, folded arms and looking tough. He smiled proudly. He then showed them one of his father with a short, bespectacled Gramsci.

'This one has Edward in it.' He pointed to yet another shot of his father gripping a flag of some sort, this time with a tall, slim and smiling Edward Lazen by his side. The shape of his head was instantly familiar.

'He was interested in everything; when and where they were taken, the comrades, the *manifestazione,* the *polizia,* I'm afraid I was indulgent.' He smiled broadly. 'I told him about myself and the '68 protests and nearly everything I could remember from my father. I think he enjoyed it, though. He seems a nice man.'

'He is.' said Hanna, and asked if he knew where their friend was going after he left. He had no idea, but assumed he was returning to the Capital. He then belatedly told them that his name was Matteo and invited them to stay for a meal. James looked at

CHAPTER FOUR

her; she shook her head slightly. They declined, thanked him for his hospitality and left, their host raising a loose fist and saying, *'Combattere la buona batteglia.'* before closing his door.

Walking back to Via Borra James asked her how she felt.

'Maybe Karl's happier now; back to something he's interested in, involved in, though I can't really see him protesting and fighting with the Carabiniere, can you?'

'No, but better than going on a drinks, drugs and debauchery trail.'

'He wouldn't have done that.'

'I know, but there were a few damaging things he could have. This is solid, it's more community based, it's about people having a common enemy; the status quo. If people share a salient frame of reference that they see as hostile they tend to bond, a sort of family.' As they walked on he wondered how real it all was for Lazen.

'I still feel, though, that there's something not good about it all. I'm wondering also if you would be here if it wasn't to be with me. I'm glad you are, of course, but how far does your professional interest stretch? Would you be here?'

It was a difficult question. His immediate response, perhaps, would have been no, but he hadn't yet worked out why Lazen was still paying him.

'A bit of both; you and my job.' She squeezed his arm. He suggested they do something, 'Have a drink, relax. We have time before the train.'

As the temperature dropped she put on a shawl she'd been carrying tied round her waist and they walked across the Piazza dei Domenicani and caught a bus to the seaside boardwalk. They had lunch and an ice cream at a gelato, its taste reminding him of Della Mura's ice cream shop on the corner of his childhood street in Plaistow, while he made a few jokes and tried to entertain her. She was rather unresponsive, pleasantly neutral. He knew he couldn't walk about with her much longer trying to get her to share his interest in the place; it seemed pretty obvious that she wanted to see whether Lazen had returned to Rome.

She slept in the seat opposite him on the return journey, the side of her head against the window, her mouth closed, hardly seeming to breathe. There were people around them in the carriage, but as it grew dark and the train's lights came on there appeared to be a slightly brighter light above her seat, making her auburn hair look darker and shinier, her smooth face at peace. She turned her head outwards towards the window more, cheek touching the glass. She sleepily raised a leg to rest on a knee, her shoeless foot pointing down, moving slightly with the motion of the train. He looked out of the window, saw his own unpleasing reflection, and wondered what would happen between them.

It had gone midnight when they got back to the hotel, he having rung the concierge as they'd left Livorno to hold rooms for them. They were the same ones; away from each other.

He awoke at six thinking of a television drama he'd watched a few evenings before leaving London in which most of the interior shots showed characters eating or drinking, and had perversely decided to list the number of times in a week of dramas where similar shots occurred and, while he was at it, note the amount of commercials, not necessarily for things to eat, showing close ups of food entering mouths. He then wondered whether his intense dislike of this was the legacy of the Victorianism entrenched in his working class parents that emphasised, as a result of religion and power, the importance of manners and virtues over bodily functions; almost a reluctant admission that we had a body. But if realism was the aim of the scenes, why not, he thought, show characters farting, pissing and shitting.

Aware he was descending into the ridiculous, and also tiring himself, he got up, showered and, assuming Hannah would knock on his door again, pushed a note between door and frame to say that he'd gone down to breakfast. After indulging on doughnuts and hot chocolate while watching the day grow brighter, his phone pinged, It was a text from Hannah saying she wasn't well, it was a recurring viral thing that occasionally bothered her and that she'd call him later. He was disappointed. He thought of the previous day and of Matteo and his Party and had an urge to discover more of its origins. The sun flooding into the room caused him to change his mind and he went out.

Another piece of map pen-sticking at the nearest metro found

CHAPTER FOUR

him at Cornelia station. He went towards some tall trees as he left it and after a small admission price walked into the Botanical Gardens. As he started ambling around this mini piece of countryside he dismissed the idea that public gardens should exist within an ethos of strict and caring maintenance. There were few visitors, mostly young mothers pushing buggies, as he strolled through wild cacti and bamboo and under wide palms and yuccas, climbed a sloping terrace of gravelly paths, found a dusty olive grove and heard birdsong for the first time since he'd been in the city. He wanted to raise a fist in triumph when he heard an English tourist complain to her male companion that the nearby roses hadn't been dead-headed for years.

Not wishing to explore the entire acreage nor return to the same metro station, and spotting a gap in a broken fence panel behind some juniper trees, his little boy joy of doing something slightly forbidden returned and he climbed through the gap and slid down a grassy incline to a road. He walked for a few minutes then turned into a wider, tree-lined thoroughfare and was going past a Milanese fashion shop when he saw a familiar figure on the sidewalk in front of him. It was the long, flowing coat that he recognised, but this time without the hat. Its wearer was bending his head slightly down towards a dark-haired woman next to him dressed mostly in red, including her high heeled shoes. She turned her face and its dark eyes and laughing mouth towards Lazen.

James slowed his steps. Was this another staged cameo, someone else he'd persuaded or bought to act another part for him? But as this was without a captive audience in a prescribed space would he get the same satisfaction? Or perhaps it wasn't a scenario after all, maybe it was just an attractive man and woman who had, or were hoping to have, a satisfying relationship. He knew, of course, that Lazen couldn't do this; perhaps having a desire to fall in love, but not in it. He didn't know what to do. He decided to follow them, but this time there was no invite. He was now, overtly, a voyeur.

He didn't have to remain behind them for long. Lazen put his arm around her waist, briefly pulling her towards him and leading them into a caffe. It was a small one and James couldn't go in without being seen. He retreated a few yards and stood in the doorway of a butchers shop, impatiently looking around him and alternately seeing if he could name the different cuts of meat though its window and counting the number of Fiat cars that went by. He occasionally poked his head out to see if they were leaving. They came out after a while and walked across to a bus stop. A bus came almost immediately. Another quandary. His embarrassment deepened as, seeing them move to the back seats, he forced himself to jump on as the doors were closing. He paid the driver and sat just behind him, pulling his jacket collar up and looking steadfastly out the window. People got on as the vehicle called at more stops; someone sitting on the seat next to him made him feel less visible. Keeping a peripheral eye on the folding doors he saw them, a mere metre away, manoeuvre past the standing passengers and leave the vehicle as it stopped. He squeezed out after them into a wedge of people and watched them cross the road. It was getting dark, the street lights beginning to cone on. He crossed after them and into an area of low, concrete post-war buildings with small, sparse courtyard gardens which seemed to be full of dogs. They walked fifty metres in front of him, holding hands and occasionally turning to each other, along roads named Gardenia or Chestnut Street; James seeing little sign of botany.

They stopped. He gently stepped behind a cracked concrete cycle shed, hearing the girl say, with a strong Italian accent, 'I'll leave you now; you know my mother's coming, anyway.'

Lazen kissed her on the lips and walked away, holding his hand up in that familiar, slight wave. He went by James, back across the road and with that lazy, relaxed manner hailed a taxi, climbed in and was driven off. James stood there. He'd lost him.

He turned to look in the direction of the girl. She was heading towards three youths, two wearing hoods, who had started fighting each other in the centre of the road. She halted, spread her arms and shouted, 'Hey, *fermalo, questa e casa mia. No vivo qui, fermalo. per favore.*' Then, just as loudly and in what James guessed was a repetition, 'Stop it, it's my home, you musn't do this. Stop it, please.'

They stood still and looked at her. 'Oh, this place, *malformato.* She shook her head. *'Voi extra comunitare.'*

CHAPTER FOUR

'I was born here.' said one of them in an African accent.

She held her arms up, hands outwards. *'Scusi, scusi,* I'm, sorry.'

He walked towards her. James moved nearer, frightened for her.

'You live here? We haven't seen you before.'

'I haven't been here long.'

'Okay, we will escort you.' He beckoned to the others. 'It's alright, *bene.*

Letting her lead they walked on either side of her, James moving quietly behind them for a while longer. He could hear them talking and laughing, one playfully pushing another till she turned her head and said something in Italian whereupon they stopped. A little after, he could see them in the growing dark silhouetted by a porch light as they said goodbye to her and she went into her house. As he started walking away they ran by him, one shouting, *'Buonanotte signore.'*

He took a disappointingly English looking bus back to the hotel and thought that perhaps it was time for Lazen to see him again. The angry resentment the latter had felt towards him was, perhaps, being pushed away, the emotional space it had occupied now being filled with the girl. He rang Hannah as he got off the bus.

'I was about to call you, I'm feeling a little better. Do you want to come and see me?' She asked him to bring a machiatto from the bar.

She looked pale and smiled a little weakly as she opened her door. She was wearing a dressing gown.

'You've only got the one, want to share with me?'

He sat with her around a small glass table. Sipping the thick, dark coffee with her would have been pleasant if he wasn't having a debate with himself about whether to tell her he'd seen Lazen with a woman. He didn't really want to see her reaction. He wanted it to be relief, but didn't wish to look into her eyes and see, perhaps, hurt, and a lost sort of anger.

'What have you been doing today?'

He told her, but didn't mention the woman. 'I actually followed him,' he said lightly, 'but he went into this housing estate and then jumped into a taxi. I lost him, I'm afraid, but he's alive and looked well,'

'What are the odds, eh?' She seemed to have a little more energy suddenly, her smile stronger. She asked him what the Gardens had been like, but he sensed the feigned interest.

He felt like an adolescent as he almost blurted out, 'You don't seem to have been with me since we left Paris. You - '

'I couldn't have come anywhere today, I told you.'

'No, emotionally, and not just preoccupied, you've been a little distant, reserved.'

'Have I? I'm sorry.' He could almost hear a sympathetic, earth mother, 'Aah,' as she leant forward and lightly brushed the side of his face with her hand. 'I'll make it up to you.' She raised her eyebrows. 'It's getting late now.'

He stood. She kissed his cheek. 'Goodnight. See you in the morning.'

His note was still on the door as he entered his room.

CHAPTER 5

He had been up for a while, waiting for her to knock. When she did she looked better, but he knew she was still concerned about not knowing where Lazen was.

'Shall we be touristy?' she asked after a quiet breakfast.

He asked her where she would like to go. Never having been to the city before, she wanted to see the Coliseum.

Leaning on the rails with two hundred other sightseers admiring its size and the feat of its construction, James said, 'Call me insensitive if you will, but I have no feeling of awe for this place; for me it means slave labour, a periodic opiate for the masses, Russell Crowe and Ridley Scott's digitalized lions.'

'I felt a little flat, too,' she said, as they walked down the ancient steps to leave, 'maybe I've seen too many pictures of it.'

'Similar to when I first saw Picasso's 'Guernica' in Madrid, it seemed merely another reproduction.'

'Maybe it's best seen lit at night; the glow through the arches, that huge silhouette against a deep indigo sky. Romantic, eh?' She laughed, 'Let's go somewhere else.'

They went to a nearby restaurant where the nearest to a classic Italian dish he could manage was a carbonara and an affagato. After they'd eaten he asked her what accents she'd had to adopt on stage. She mimicked the only four she'd done. Attempting to amuse her he tried a few, especially those requiring little subtlety.

'You're pretty good.'

'But not as good Karl?'

She smiled. He wished he hadn't said it, it implied something competitive between him and Lazen. He pushed away the image of her laughing at the latter's jokes in the bars, quickly convincing himself that it had been part of their act. He tried out a joke on her, covering up its lukewarm response by explaining that the function of sick jokes was to create an escape from stark reality, the stereotypical battle axe mother-in-law being just one.

'Wouldn't that also be useful in preventing her being a sex object to her daughter's husband?' She leant forward across the

table. 'And don't try so hard.'
'Where else would you like to go?'
'Would St. Peter's Basilica be too heavy for you? We've never talked about god have we.'
'Why should we?'
'You've confirmed my intuition.'
'What about a compromise? I saw the name recently; St. Andrea Della Velle. That okay?'

They caught a jolting, swaying bus crowded with builders, nuns and children with the end not justifying the means. The size, the paintings, the gold leaf was too rich for the aesthetic imbibed from the protestant churches his parentally imposed childhood visits for births deaths and marriages had taken him. He stayed there, feeling pressed gradually flat. She seemed to enjoy the place.

They walked around a little more, had supper then returned to the hotel and had a drink at the bar. He walked with her to her room. She stopped and turned to him, kissing him on the mouth and, as he started to respond, pulled away.

'Goodnight, again. I enjoyed today.'

He went to bed feeling frustrated and a little lonely, but forced his professionalism to consider Lazen. What would he think of a religious god? A god, for him, would have nothing to do with churches or morality; that would be a false god, like his father was, perhaps. But where *was* his client?'

After a restless sleep he woke early again and sent a text telling Hannah he'd be in the breakfast room. He was the first diner there and as he sat waiting a woman walked through carrying bedding. Someone poked their head around the door and called, 'Sara.' to which she replied with, *'Un momento'* and let some pillow slips drop to the floor. James picked them up, placed them on top of her pile and, remembering the name, asked her if she also worked at the l'Angelique.

'*Grazie*. That's me, I do shifts in both places.'

'You know Luca then?'

She frowned. 'You are the English man looking for *amico?*'

'Yes.'

'I think Luca wanted to tell you *amico* is with him at Piazza del

CHAPTER FIVE

Popolo today. Who knows? He is will o' the wisp, you say. It's more *proteste*. They will give Luca sack one day. *Ciao, madam,*' she said to Hannah as she came in and she, herself, left the room.

'What was she saying to you?' Hanna asked, sitting down at his table. He told her.

'Perhaps it's the season for protests. Will we be able to see him? Will there be a lot of people there?' 'You do want to go, don't you?'

'In what order do I answer?'

'I'm not sure if I really want to see him if he's just one of a crowd.'

'You prefer to see him on his own to make sure he doesn't bear a grudge?' She didn't answer.

'I'm aware this is beginning to sound like 'Any Questions,' but are you going to tell me what it was that he bought you?'

'No. What time is this thing supposed to start?'

'Today, sometime. I don't know precisely when.' She suggested they make their way to the square as soon as they'd eaten.

They took a short metro ride to Piazza Venetia then walked through Via del Corso where he tried without success to tempt her to a quick walk through its meandering alleys, admiring her restraint as she glanced only briefly at fashion shop windows; Armani, Dadada and Zara having to do without her. Spotting a notice in English saying that the Palazzo Doria Pamphilj was closed, he told her he'd like to see its gallery some time and that she'd like it, too. She nodded absently. They passed straggles of people and solitary groups waiting on the kerbs and stood at the corner of the square. He noticed a small gallery behind them.

'Let's go in for a while, we won't miss him,' She looked at him a little suspiciously. 'Suppose we do? There may be thousands here.'

'We can't do anything about that.'

Inside were mainly landscapes, mostly, it seemed, in the style of Constable which, although just about appropriate for the Italian countryside, the Lowry-like stick men in the other paintings looked somewhat incongruous walking through Vatican City. They heard more people outside, left the gallery and walked to the edge of the sidewalk.

The sound seemed to begin quickly and just as quickly swell. Three hundred or so people entered the square singing and shouting then a wide, long band of people marched in with Lazen in the centre of the leading line chanting in unison with the others. James noticed that slight hesitation again before lifting a foot at the start of each step. His eyes were fixed ahead, his shoulders back, thick hair over the neck of his sweater, occasionally looking upwards and punching the air, almost turning the large wedge of marchers behind him into a phalanx with him at its head. Here was a kind of glory. The girl who had been with him two evenings previously was next but one to him, with Luca towards the far end of the front rank. As he watched him, James wondered whether, despite appearances, Lazen was struggling to feel a genuine, solid sense of belonging under the adrenalin rush. He looked at Hannah. She seemed mesmerised.

A mass of people then swept in chanting *Lotta dura senza paura,* the shouting and sporadic singing harsher, louder. Large groups of people, mostly young, mainly students entered, a national flag stretched around them. As people on the sidewalks moved into the swirl, Hannah was knocked into and nearly fell before James grabbed her and pulled her into a doorway next to the gallery. Almost immediately the space was filled by other escapees. Spotting some steps at the side of the building leading into a basement area full of dustbins and crates, they hurried down. She looked startled then grinned at him.

'Gosh, that was so quick, everybody just coming into the square. There must be thousands now.'

James was momentarily filled with pleasure, the 'Gosh' was so old fashioned; English, innocent, schoolgirl. He suddenly warmed to Buckinghamshire.

A man came out of a door next to the rubbish. *'Tutto bene?'* He looked a little concerned and beckoned them to go through to a passage. *'Venire.'* He pointed to the stairs and they followed him up three flights of them. He turned into a landing then a large front room and pointed at the window. *'Si vedio meglio qui.'* The view was certainly better. The three of them stood there looking out, James feeling that he was in a private box at a stadium. As

CHAPTER FIVE

Lazen and his group moved on they were followed and increasingly surrounded by the crowd as more demonstrators came noisily into the quickly filling area. There were banners, some written in English as well as Italian saying, 'Give us Jobs.' and 'Find A Way Back.' a smaller one saying, 'Italy A Slave To Jewish Banks.' Another, 'We Don't Need The Fat Cows' *'Non Abbamo Bisogne Vacche Gras.'* and a large one with 'Get Rid Of The Pigs' scrawled across it.

They then heard the synthesized wail of a siren as a police wagon pushed its way through the crowd towards the far end of the square where some black shirted, white belted police, who James had noticed dotted at intervals on the kerbs, pushed into the front of the marchers. They grabbed some of them, including Lazen and the girl, and pulled them towards the kerb. James could just see Lazen with his arm protectively around the girl's head as the siren reached a crescendo then stopped. They and several others were pushed into the wagon which, its ridiculously tuneful bleating starting again, pulled away then forced itself through the crowd into a side road and disappeared.

It had happened quickly. He wasn't sure how much she'd seen of Lazen being arrested. They watched for a while longer. There didn't appear to be any more arrests. The crowd's sporadic chanting and yelling became louder for a few minutes then gradually quietened as it moved slowly through the square towards the thoroughfare at the end. The shopkeeper turned his head to them and shrugged. *'Finire presto.'* They thanked him for his hospitality, went out up the steps into the slowly moving mass and moved along with them.

'I didn't really see, but did they arrest some people?' She had to raise her voice to be heard. He wasn't sure how much to tell her; again apprehensive about her reaction. He felt a little Machiavellian.

'They did, and it could have been Karl, also, but if it was him, they'll release him soon, it's probably happened to him before, anyway.'

She turned sharply to him. 'Why? Is he some sort of criminal?'

'No, but the police work for the state, they're paid to protect it.'

They carried on in silence. 'He'll be okay, maybe Luca is with him, he shouldn't be there long, he's probably used to spending some post demo time in a cell, anyway.'

As the crowd thinned it moved a little quicker. They were turning out of the square before she said, 'I think we should go to the police.'

He felt impatient with her; wanted suddenly to get this job, this project over with, no hindrances, no obstacles, wanted her to be with him, not part of her wanting to be somewhere else, with someone else.

'Okay, we'll try to find him; you can give him your sympathy vote.' He held his hands up. 'Sorry, you didn't deserve that. The question is, how are we going to find him?'

He looked around him, there were few police visible. Seeing a nearby marcher relinquish one end of a banner and walk away from a group of others, James asked him if he spoke English.

'No, ma lui fa.' he said, pointing to someone in the group.

James went over to him and, utilising most of his Italian vocabulary, began with, *'Mi scusi, no parla Italiano, mi dispiace,'* and asked where the police were likely to take arrested demonstrators. He was told that it was usually the police station off Via Cavour, a short, crowded metro trip away. They journeyed there in silence.

Under a large, brash 'Polizia di Stato' sign two armed police at the entrance asked them what they wanted. James told them and they were taken into the building and asked to sit at the end of a counter where people were asking for help or information. They waited a few minutes and stood as a sergeant came and informed them that the man they wanted was there, but only one of them could be admitted into his cell and for the maximum of half an hour.

'Perhaps you should see him, you're the professional. He needs you.' She seemed to say this last a little reluctantly. She turned to the officer. 'Where is the nearest place I can wait; a caffe or somewhere?'

He told her where to go. She gave James a quick look which he couldn't quite decipher then left through the double doors of the entrance.

The cells were in the basement. The policeman accompanying

him turned the key in the door, nodded to its occupant and left. Lazen was half sitting, half lying on a bunk with a languid urbanity more suited to the L'Angelique than a police cell. He seemed surprised for only a second when James stepped in.

'You have come to me then. How did you find me?'

James explained that Hannah had guessed that he was at his favourite hotel, that they had gone there and accidentally met Luca. There was a chair opposite the bunk. Lazen gestured for him to sit. James looked at him and said firmly,

'I want you to understand that Hanna and I are not sleeping together.'

'I should think that would be the last thing you'd do, sleep. I prefer 'sexual congress.''

'We're not indulging in that either and I'm sorry if you thought otherwise. You may or may not feel you have psychological ownership of her and, although that feeling may be more intense in you than in most people in a relationship of some sort, nevertheless, you don't have any claims on her. I want you to realise that, I want you to be *in* the world.'

He knew that he should have used Lazen's first name; the familiarity, informality may have registered more, but he couldn't quite bring himself to. Lazen looked at him without expression.

'Do you want me to stay?' James asked, 'Do you still want to see me?' There was a barely perceptible nod.

'I saw you being arrested, I was there.' Even as he said it he wasn't sure why he hadn't used 'we.' 'I wondered why you were; it seemed a relatively peaceful demonstration.'

'Oh, it was merely token, they had to be seen to be doing something this time. In Turin recently some of the police removed their helmets in sympathy with the protesters. Certainly not like the old days.'

'I didn't realise you were so political.'

'Everything is politics; it's not just about elections, coups and assassinations, it's about individuals or groups that have power or potential power over other groups and individuals. A father telling his teenage daughter that she must be home by eleven is a political act.'

He stood and went to the barred window and looked out. James had often seen him look out of widows, but not one with views from a cell. He turned to James and enthusiastically asked if he knew much about Marx.

'A little. Apparently it didn't work too well in Russia.'

Lazen sat on the bed again and said wearily, 'It was hardly utopian Marxism, it was essentially state capitalism. Marx was about socialism in a land of plenty; essentially the Bolshevik revolution was forced because there was widespread poverty and hunger.'

'Sorry, my comment was rather a lazy one. Tell me about the Italian Communist party.'

'Well, since '21 it mutated into the PCI then there was the Democratica di Sinistra, now it's the Partito Democratica; who knows what it will be tomorrow.' The enthusiasm had returned. 'But the core has always been communistic, though now we have a different generation who want employment and are against the austerity measures and tax hikes. I wonder,' he mused, 'if economic growth is an inevitable corollary of capitalism. And there's recently been the Pitchfork movement: farmers, students, environmental activists, ultras, football fans like the Romanisti and laziali. At one time the communist party would have fought against fascist ultras.' He shrugged, 'Times change. My grandfather, I've just discovered, was a Marxist. I met an old man recently whose father knew him.' He took a deep breath and looked at James a little shyly. 'I have a girl friend.' James waited for him to continue. 'In fact, she's four cells from here. Luca's here, too, amongst others. We'll all be let out soon I think.'

'I guess you could actually buy your way out; somebody did tell me that corruption in Italy has been raised to an art form.'

'Italians also have a weakness for rhetoric.'

James sensed that he wanted to talk about the girl. He asked about her.

'If you knew her you probably wouldn't believe what she's currently doing for a living. She works in a club.' He forced a smile. 'She's a striptease artist. She worked in some bars when a student at Roma Tre University, she read politics. I met her on a demo about six months ago. She liked working in them, they were congenial, the tips were good. Then she worked in a couple of

CHAPTER FIVE

clubs and sort of graduated to... entertaining.' He looked quickly at James. 'The clubs are run on very strict lines; the girls musn't be touched.'

It was the old fashioned term for stripper that amused James, he'd probably used it to add some respectability to what she was doing.

'Do you want to tell me what you've been feeling since I last saw you?'

Lazen thought for a moment. 'When I'm in a protest, when I'm marching, it's so...'

'You belong.'

'Yes, we're for a cause, or causes, we're as one, we're together, doing something and, sometimes, if there's enough dissent it can work.'

'And you also have an audience.'

'Yes, of course, there's that, too.'

'When you're in front of them are you acting?'

He looked at James as if impressed by the question. 'Well, I'm aware of myself, yes, but t his time it feels... better. It's - '

'Almost real?'

He gave a rueful grin and metaphorically rubbed his hands together. 'Maybe, maybe.'

'You enjoy carrying a banner, don't you, you're saying, or trying to say, 'This is *me*.''

'Yes,' he said, clenching a fist. 'Yes.'

'And the girl?'

He looked surprised for a second. 'We share things; beliefs, ideology, she likes - '

'And the men in the club, how do you feel about them?'

He hesitated. 'We've talked for quite a while haven't we. You're not allowed to stay for long.'

'The half hour's not up yet.'

He stood. 'It's a maximum time.' He went to the door. *'Guardia, Vuoi adesso Signore Kent lasciatre, per favore?'* He turned to James. 'Thank you for coming.'

As the door was unlocked James brushed past him and smiled. 'Like old times.' Lazen averted his eyes.

'We'll see each other again.' James heard as he walked away

down the corridor.

As he signed himself out he asked the sergeant how long Lazen would be held for. He was told it would be just a few more hours. He rang Hannah as he left the building. She told him she was in a caffé nearby. As he walked to it he wondered why Lazen hadn't offered to give the girl money so she wouldn't have to do what she was doing. Perhaps he had and it had been refused because she liked doing it.

He sat down next to her wondering if the first question would be whether Lazen had asked about her. It wasn't.

'Is he alright?

'Yes, he's taking it well, should be free in a little while.'

'And professionally? Sorry, I shan't ask you that again. Has he forgiven us? What did you tell him?'

'That he'd got it wrong.'

'Did he believe you?'

'I don't know.'

'To use a cliché, perhaps he can move on now.' She paused. 'I don't know, maybe I should see him. Did he tell you where he's staying?'

'No.' He hadn't asked. In effect, he'd lost him again.

'If he's okay, about me anyway, then there's no real need for me to be here, I suppose.'

He didn't know whether she meant it or had said it to elicit a response. He hoped it was the latter. He told her he had to stay; he was being effectively funded by two sources and needed to present his research, about which he'd so far written nothing, and also to help his client. He changed the subject.

'Do you know how your understudy's faring?'

'Apparently, she vomited before going on the first night, but now she's loving it.'

'I want you to stay.'

She looked down for an instant and nodded.

He hadn't eaten since breakfast and suggested they find a restaurant. She told him she'd just had a meal and the food was fine where they were. He ordered and in between her telling him her impressions of Rome and he offering relatively uninformed opinions on Italian politics, he felt, strangely, he was dining

CHAPTER FIVE

alone.

The proprietor closed the door as the first chill of dusk came in and James suggested the Victor Emmanuel Monument if she fancied some classical bits of the city.

'No, I'm tired, really, you can go, though.'

He didn't want to. They returned to their hotel and walked up the stairs to their floor. It was at the top of them that she asked whether Lazen had enquired about her. He should have told her that he hadn't, not only because it was true, but it may have created in her a perception of Lazen not caring for her. Feeling immediately guilty in his awareness that this would suit him, he told her that he had. She kissed him quickly on the cheek again.

'Do you mind? I'll make it up to you, I promise.'

She went towards her room. He sat in the empty bar with a drink for a while, the strains of 'Set 'em up, Joe,' momentarily settling in his head.

After scribbling a few rather clumsily written observations in his room, he got ready for bed and thought that if there was more than just fondness for Lazen in Hannah, then to see him for the first time in Rome as she had done, effectively leading a mass of people in an anti-autocratic protest, like an Anthony perhaps, it would have intensified whatever it was that she felt for him.

CHAPTER 6

He rang Luca as soon as he'd showered. They'd all been let out around midnight none the worse for their experience, though most of them had been through it before. Luca's sister had briefly looked in on them and spent some time with the girl. 'She is a good friend of Gradia's, they were students together; she's a lawyer now. She doesn't come on marches with us, but her heart's in the right place and she's great at arguing with the *polizia.*'

James asked him where Lazen was staying.

'I'm not sure I'm supposed to tell you; he gets like this at times, he's wary about certain things. He'll contact you if he needs to. I hope he does. Did you see the old man?' James briefly described the visit.

'You should come to the 'Bida Bang' one evening and see Gradia and the girls, all good, clean, dirty fun. Karl's been, but he's a bit uptight there. *Ciao,* Mister Kent.'

The first thing she asked when she entered his room was if he'd contacted Luca to see if he knew where Lazen was. He gave a summary of what had been said.

'He'll contact me, Hannah.'

'You rarely use my name.'

'Ditto.'

She stepped toward him and gave him a mock bite on the side of his neck. 'Are you ready? Where shall we go? It's alright, I know where; Audrey Hepburn and the Spanish Steps.'

'All glamorous hairdressers, taxi drivers and the most boring man in Hollywood.'

'Let's go.' She was out the door before he had his jacket on.

After another brief metro ride they climbed the steps eating an obligatory gelato then, after she realised that the Via Margutta was now home to antique shops and artists and not the film's hero, they utilised the trams and trains of the city's ubiquitous transport system to get to the Milvian Bridge. They walked across it, stopping halfway to look at the view and the Tiber.

'How about hailing a taxi, getting inside it then out again and run across the road to me. You're wearing jeans and not the long dress, but that'll have to do.'

She laughed and said, 'It's not Paris though, is it.' She stretched her body forward from the waist to see how far under the bridge she could see. She straightened. 'It's pleasant here.'

He laid an arm casually around her shoulder as if he had done so a thousand times before.

She grinned. 'Let's have a race.'

She started running towards the end of the bridge, he following her. He caught her at the arch just before bridge became road and leaned against the stone balustrade, panting.

'You gained a short head victory.'

She stood there, grinning, taking deep breaths. 'Shall we walk some more?'

They walked around a few roads; houses with front gardens, an olive tree in one, cypresses in others, a palm tree and a small fountain in another. As they came onto a main road he stopped her and, gently holding her shoulders, turned her towards him.

'Come to my room after our meal?'

She smiled at him. Taking her silence as assent he held his arm out at a passing bus; surprisingly it stopped. They stood holding on to straps and watching the city get busier and noisier as they neared the centre. Spotting a hotel which reminded him of a sketch he'd made of the tapering columns of the temple of Khons at Karnak when at college, he pushed the bell button and they got off at the next stop.

It had a circular bar and tables for two set against curved walls with large windows. There were few English translations on the menu, between them picking out the salted cod, ricotta cake and gnocchi alla Romana, the latter pleasingly reminding him of school meals semolina. He looked around him at the smartly dressed couples at the bar, its subdued lighting as dusk begun, the leaves of the trees outside reflecting street lights, the food, the wine, and feeling relaxed and at last pleased that he was in Rome, and with Hannah.

She had done most of the talking, happily telling of some of the characters she'd acted with: the hams, the talented ones, the egoists, and a few dressing room tales. By the time they'd finished their desserts she had quietened. She was looking down at the table; the hiatus stretching. She looked up.

'I feel drained. It's the thing again. I was told a few years ago that viruses like this take half an hour to go through the body, but can take years to leave it. I don't get it often.' She slowly stood. 'I'm sorry.' He could see the pallor of her skin.

'Sit down, I'll get a taxi.' He got a number from the barman and after sitting silently with her for a while the vehicle arrived. She was just as silent on the short journey back. The lift wasn't working. He helped her up the stairs and took the keycard from her as she laboriously pulled it from her jeans. He touched it on the lock and asked if he could do anything. She shook her head. He kissed her forehead.

'This is such a pity.'

'I know.' she whispered, and closed the door.

He wasn't sure what to do. He didn't want to be alone in the bar again nor go out and was reluctantly accepting that he would have to do some report writing when Lazen rang.

'I don't know where you are, but do you fancy coming to the club? It's just off the Via Lamada. Gradia's here, come see her. Bring Hannah if you wish.' It seemed to James that the last was said slightly provocatively. In a mood of instant masochism he decided he may as well get even more frustrated than he felt now. He had pictures of himself telling Hannah about it: the show, Karl, the girl, and even comforting her, the tears maybe, possibly anger, the clinging to him. He erased the images, they were manipulative. He was aware that he was like a little boy trying to get his own back.

Knowing that strip clubs were illegal in Italy, the conspicuousness of the angled, red neon sign on the front of the 'Bada Bing' club surprised him. He had never been to such a place before; maybe in part it was an unthinking residual dislike of Angus McGill smut in him that had kept him away. The bouncers at the entrance were large. He went in. The walls and ceilings were red with black tables and floor, the music quiet but raunchy. There were about fifty men, their drinks being served at the tables by two girls in red looking like an amalgam of bunny

CHAPTER SIX

girls and air hostesses. It was a kind of mini theatre in the round. The performers, two blonde girls in strips of flimsy ribbon, glass-like high heeled shoes and lit by green and blue spotlights, were sensuously sliding up and down poles like snakes around an erection. 'Cabaret' seemed like an age of innocent decadence.

His client was sitting on his own at a rear table, dark jacket accentuating his hair. As James went across to him he gave a faint smile and asked what he was drinking.

'Well, this is hardly a consulting room, but I don't want to drink on the job, as it were.'

'Sit and relax, watch and tell me what you think.'

'Well, I could say the usual things; that the men are mostly married, but sex starved or their bedroom life is without adventure, meaning perhaps that the pubescent boy in them is not allowed to do what he fantasised about when he was ten, or - '

'No, don't psychologise it, feel it.' He grinned, 'Me telling you that, eh? Do the girls excite you?'

'A little, and I'm not being falsely casual, but they're a bit sterile, obvious.'

'Sex is in the head? I saw a car sticker recently with 'Philosophers do it in their heads.''

'It's also in public. You like sex in public.'

'That wasn't sex, that was acting, just - '

'Not sex, then.'

He gestured to one of the waitresses and pointed to his empty glass.

'Gradia served drinks here for a while.'

'What does she do? What they're doing?' The blondes were continuing writhing around their shiny chrome poles.

Lazen briefly looked around, bending his head upwards. 'I can understand why it's mainly red in here, but the black... black symbolises death doesn't it?'

The girls performed vertical splits, left the poles and, after an embrace and a long kiss on each others lips with the audience cheering, they ran off to a side door.

'Apparently the Japanese associate sex with death.'

'So it's not universal then? Would they see the Oedipal differently perhaps; would they have an Oedipal?'

The music changed to something slow and bluesy and, with her black hair, dark, vivid lips and a long, classically cut white dress, the girl from the housing estate entered. She turned gradually towards everyone, hands moving down from her neck, undoing buttons slowly and provocatively. She bent forward for the last one, straightened and, with a slight shrug of her shoulders, the dress slipped to the floor. Then the sound of a hybrid of orchestral and military music trumpeted out and, twirling the miniature tassels on her bikini top, she kicked out, shimmied her hips and slowly ran her hands from her breasts to below her thighs and kicked high again. She put her hands behind her and began to undo her top then, looking coquettishly over her shoulder, decided not to and started to sway around the raised dais, spinning her tassels again. Her purposely retro act seemed more at home on Prohibition era Broadway than in a strip club and with no gallery to play to she became everyone's, even the bunny girls had stopped serving to watch her. He looked at Lazen who, although seemingly entranced, was giving occasional covert glances at the men around him. James could feel his tenseness.

Gradia repeated her routine twice more, each time the backward glances more provocative, her bikini top increasingly not quite undone. When she swayed off there were cheers, clapping, whoops and then loud chatter. Lazen stared briefly at the door she'd exited and, a glint of desire in his eyes, asked James what he thought.

'She knows her stuff; the act, her expressions, the movements. Not many communists like her, eh?'

'Not many rich ones, either. There's a kind of interval now and it's much the same afterwards, though Gradia's not on again. I'm going to see her now. There's a party later, perhaps you'd like to come.'

'To observe?'

'No, join in if you like; there'll be a few of the people from the march there, maybe even a member of the *polizia.*' He laughed. 'It's okay, he's a sympathiser, tells his boss that he's undercover or something. Will you?' He wrote the address on a scrap of paper and gave it to him.

James, still aware he was feeling a little sulk because Hannah

CHAPTER SIX

was in her room alone and not with him in his, said yes.

It was, coincidentally, one of the houses on a street that he and Hannah had walked down hours previously. He could see figures in the front room. A fair haired man wearing a Che Guevara t-shirt opened the door and asked if he was the friend Karl had mentioned. The room was crowded and split loosely into groups, Lazen, drink in hand, was at the centre of one of them. The man, who James assumed was the host, brought him a drink. James stood by the door, bits of animated conversation, some in Italian, some in English surrounding him. 'Well, where else does it start? The judiciary, politics, art, science, where else but from the infrastructure?' someone was rhetorically asking. A short, middle aged woman with her back to Lazen offered, 'Culture?' Lazen turned his head towards her. 'And where does that come from? He seemed annoyed. 'I'll give you his thesis in a sentence. Our reality, consciousness, identity, our political, cultural and economic systems are determined by the ways in which we technologically transmute the physical world.'

The woman turned and said, 'You say it as if it was an absolute. Of course, we - '

'It is.' He almost shouted it. As he turned his attention back to the others he saw James and came over to him.

'Hello, I don't know how much of all this will interest you, but I'm sure some will, you can posit psychological reasons for the opinions held if you like. I'm afraid this is rather tribal, our little communistic village, but they're good people. Nils will give you what you want. He organises demonstrations and the drinks.'

James could see Gradia in a corner leaning back on a wall with three men talking to her, her eyes bright as she looked from one to the other. He could hear her saying, 'But it doesn't matter if someone recognises me on a demo. If they feel that what I do for a job devalues my politics, that's their problem, *il loro problema.*'

It seemed to him that Lazen was deliberately keeping his back to her as if he didn't want to see her with the men. Nils, bringing a drink for someone, said in a stage whisper as he passed Lazen, 'Marx did overemphasise the economic, though, don't you think?' There was no response. Someone then said with a smile,

95

'And what about the causal power of religion, family and the subjective view of individuals?' What was pretty obvious was that they were purposely provoking him with some friendly, institutionalised banter.

'Subjectivity splits all the social sciences.' Lazen said. 'If, for instance, someone doesn't feel they're exploited in terms of surplus value, are they exploited? If a manual worker thinks he's middle class, is it not true in its consequences? And if we're not going to see social generalizations as having any validity then read novels, they're often better written.' And with a quick look towards James, said, 'And if we're going to emphasize subjectivity we're moving towards the generalizations of psychology as a provider of so-called rock bottom explanations.'

Just then Luca came in, nodded to some people and shook hands with others. Gradia went over to him.

'Where's Livia? Not with you?'

'Couldn't make it; working on a case.' He noticed James. 'Mister Kent, and where is your friend?'

'She couldn't get here either.'

The girl returned to her corner, but not before giving Lazen's arm an affectionate squeeze. As James was being asked by Luca what he thought about the previous day's march, his phone rang. It was Hannah. He excused himself and went into an empty kitchen.

'Hello,' she said weakly, 'I just woke up and thought I'd say goodnight. I'm going back to sleep now. Goodnight.'

It was pleasant to hear her voice; he enjoyed a brief feeling of warmth and returned to the room. There was more noise, it was getting hotter. The conversation was largely about the demonstration. More people came in; Nils was busy passing drinks and the occasional plate of food around. James saw a chair in a corner and sat. Lazen silently mouthed for him to join in, but he was reasonably content to listen to the sound of Italian; the trilling 'r,' stresses, the fingers and thumb emphasis, and watching Gradia, who was now standing next to Lazen and vivaciously gesticulating. The host offered him another drink. James asked him where he was from.

'Sweden. It's such a stable country, so conservative, there are no challenges.' He shrugged. 'Here, there's corruption, political history, fascism, the Left; and I'm learning a third language.' Not for the first time did James feel linguistically inadequate when with the non-English.

Someone turned the music up and people began casually dancing. He watched for a while then the woman who Lazen had briefly chastised asked him to dance. He held her loosely, silently stepped and swayed and thought of Hannah. The tempo changed, he thanked her and sat again. The talk, the laughter grew louder. He decided to leave. He looked around for his client, but couldn't see him. He then asked Nils, who seemed to be everywhere at the same time, where the toilet was. He pointed up the stairs. After using it he passed a door that was ajar. Spotting what he thought was the same wallpaper as in his Paris hotel room he gently pushed the door. It swung open. He automatically reacted to a movement in the half dark and saw on a bed a black laced corset, vertically striped stockings and long black hair, all belonging to Gradia. Lying next to her, his back to James and his surprisingly well muscled body stripped to its boxer shorts, was Lazen. Despite feeling for a second that he'd stepped into a Feydeau farce, James knew that any notion he may have held that the two of them had merely been inhabiting Lazen-created cameos was rendered invalid. He closed the door quickly, went down the stairs and, briefly hearing Nils' goodbye to him, left the house.

Waking from images of corsets, stockings, red tassels and the cabbage rose patterned wallpaper of his parents' living room sliding through his sleep, and not wanting to disturb Hanna by calling, he sent her a text. He then tried again to begin a report for Morgan.

This man, who has been my client for some three weeks, has had irregular, but, on average, almost daily contact with me. He…

He what? Has embroiled himself in Italian politics, found a woman, while another, who just may be yearning for him, has been accompanying the writer in order to offer companionship, frustration and disappointment? He went down to breakfast then out into a bright, autumnal sun.

He walked aimlessly around for a while, though an almost subliminal aim perhaps was to see if he really could catch a glimpse of Sylvano Mangano and a sun drenched balcony somewhere, and then took some random bus rides, having little idea where he was. Knowing that you could never really get lost in a city, even if not understanding its spoken language, he felt quite at ease; except for the anticipation of Hannah's reaction to his account of some of last night's entertainment. After another few hours of disinterested roaming he returned to his room. She called him. 'Where are you? Good, I'll be there.'

He had to work out what to tell her about the evening. An army of vested interests marched into him, but compromising as honestly as he could, he decided to tell her about the club only.

She stepped lightly in announcing she felt better, 'I think it's gone now; I don't want it again. I'm actually hungry. What did you do last evening?' He told her about the club.

'What were they wearing? What was the music like? Just men there?'

He answered as best he could, telling her he'd left before it had finished. She frowned.

'I can't really imagine him there. Anyway, let's go.'

The breakfast room also served light lunches. It was a rather silent meal. When they'd finished she asked him what Lazen's reaction to the girls had been.

'He just watched them and clapped like everyone else. I shouldn't think they were the best of their type.'

'I bet he liked the vaudeville one, he'd go for an act like that.'

He didn't answer and was about to ask if there was anywhere she fancied visiting when Luca appeared in front of them.

'*Mangiare bene,* whenever I see you you're eating.' He looked at Hannah. 'Are you enjoying Rome? She nodded. 'Your friend Karl certainly is.' He looked from her to James. 'Eh, Mister Kent?' He glanced back at her. 'Perhaps he didn't tell you. The party?' He turned to James. 'I think you may have left, but him and Gradia; how about that?' James could see her concentrating on every word.

'I think they'd been upstairs; nudge, nudge, wink, wink, as you

CHAPTER SIX

say. She came back in the room and you knew something had gone on. I didn't see him.' He shook his head. 'She asked Nils for a particular piece of music then started mimicking her club act, but fully clothed of course. Everyone loved it; the way she moved... you know. Then Livia, my sister, came and she and Gradia left. It went on a while after that. I still have a headache. Again, I must go, more work; another day, another Euro. I'm off to the L' Angelique now, it's outside my area, really, but they're always calling me. Oh, and they're thinking of opening another club; the 'Bada Boom,' what else? *Ciao.*'

He was probably still in earshot when she said, 'You didn't tell me about the party or the girl.' She raised her voice. 'Is this more lies? Sins of omission again?'

'Look... I'm not sure, even now, what you feel for Lazen. Alright, you're fond of him, but I've felt for a while it's more than that. Let's go outside.' He pointed to a window behind the reception counter. 'There's a small garden at the back.'

They went through a rear exit and sat on a bench. 'I was going to tell you that the girl was another bit of playacting, but it obviously isn't. I didn't want to tell you because I thought you'd be hurt and you'd realise perhaps that you'd been used, interesting and enjoyable as it may have been and that really you were just one amongst quite a few others, as I think you've known from the beginning. I was, if you like, protecting you, but you need to face - '

'I'm not your client, *he* is. Don't use your professional energy up on me.'

He was unsure from her expression what she thought or felt. She stood, grabbed his wrist and began pulling him up. 'Come with me.' He followed her back through the foyer, up the stairs and along the corridor. She went into her room and, grabbing his wrist again, pulled him inside, telling him to close the door. She sat on the end of the bed looking lost. Then she kicked off her shoes and jumped on the bed, facing him. She put her hands inside the waist of her jeans and slowly pulled up her blouse.

'You wanna see a stripper? How's this?'

She began exaggeratedly rotating her hips while undoing the buttons, pulling the shirt off a little too quickly for it to be part of a stage routine. Putting her arms behind her she loosened her bra, letting it fall on the sheets. His initial puzzlement at what she was doing turned to excitement as she stood there, legs apart, showing him her breasts almost defiantly. She undid the button at the waist of her jeans and slowly unzipped the fly. Putting her outstretched hands inside them she worked them down her thighs till they dropped around her feet. She kicked them away from her then exaggeratedly swayed her hips again as the fingers of both hands went inside her knickers.

'This is me making it up to you, baby. Wanna give me some special Joe treatment?' She pushed her forefingers into her crotch then quickly pulled them out and held her drooping hands high above her head. She flicked her fingers towards him. 'I'm a viper, I have forked tongue. Ssss.'

He took a step towards her then stopped. He was simultaneously aroused and repulsed. He knew that she was doing this not for him, but Lazen. It was as if Lazen was in front of her. He wanted to slap her. He shouted. 'Stop it.' She did immediately. Looking down at him, she put her hands on the side of her face and began to cry. He stepped to the side of the bed and held his arms up. She almost fell into them. They stood there a while, he loosely holding her.

He barely heard her whispered, 'Go away.' He hesitated then strode to the door. He stopped himself from slamming it behind him and just stood there, looking at its melamine veneer and chrome room number. He felt a conflict of emotions: anger desire, hurt and an urge to go back inside and hold her again. He passed his room and went to go in, but, visualising the expensive pen given him by an ex-patient lying on virgin sheets of A4, decided he didn't want to tell Morgan anything about his client, didn't want to tell him anything about anything; about European cities, hotels, gardens, glass shoes, bridges, mobs... He went downstairs and out into the early evening trying to turn what he was feeing into something more mature and responsible. He wondered where Lazen was and assumed he was back in a hotel. Perhaps it was still the L' Angelique.

Trying to use increased blood flow to wipe away his mood, he made his way there on foot, aware that part of the reason was to see a little more art deco, shaken as he was. Maybe he'd go up the main staircase and admire its marble and curved wooden handrails, come down on the thirties elevator, perhaps chat to a page boy with uniform and pillbox hat. He also thought Luca might still be there.

He got to the hotel and went through into the foyer. The staircase wasn't quite as grand as he'd pictured, but the sunburst styled lift doors were. His aesthetic appreciation of those on the second floor was cut short as they were pulled open by Luca carrying some tools.

'Mr Kent.'

'We must stop meeting like this.'

'I'm not surprised at seeing you again.' He looked down at the tools. 'Some hands-on stuff here, I've used a screw, a bolt and a piece of wire. I was thinking of calling you.' He looked around him. 'People will hear us, come with me a moment.'

He went down the stairs at the side of the lift, James following, and entered some sort of store room, switching on the light as he closed the door behind them.

'It's Karl. When Livia and Gradia left last night they went back to my sister's place. Gradia cried because she felt guilty about the dance she'd done at the party. She was a little drunk, I think. It was also because when she and Karl were in the room upstairs, apparently he hadn't... couldn't do it. Maybe it was because there were people around or something, I don't know. She felt bad about it. Livia told her that it wasn't her fault and that these things happen. A short while ago, though, Karl called me to say he was going home. That's all he said. I didn't have a chance to reply, he rang off. I don't know whether he's told Gradia, I assume he has, I doubt he'd just go. It's a pity, I'll miss him. A lot of us will.' He looked quizzically at James. 'Should I have told you this? I feel you are *simpatico*, otherwise I wouldn't have.'

'I'm glad you did. Where would 'home' be, d'you think?'

He shrugged 'London, I suppose. But he'll contact me eventually, I'm sure. There's another demo, probably next month, it's in Livorno too, I can't imagine him not being there.' He looked at his watch. 'I have a night job; as ever, I need to go.' He pointed to a door at the back of the room. 'I go this way; I can park the car at the rear.'

'I'll come with you, I'm going nowhere.'

Next to the pavement outside the exit was a red Audi. Luca gestured towards it. 'This was Karl's, he had someone drive it from Paris a few days ago. It's some present, eh? He's very generous. I hope he's okay.' He climbed into it. 'We shall have a drink one day. *Ciao.*'

As James watched it screech around a corner, he knew that Lazen's failure was little to do with circumstances, the hurry, the people. Wherever it had been he couldn't have made love to Gradia. And he probably hadn't told her that he was leaving.

Seeing a small park at the end of the street he went into it. He hazarded a guess that she may have represented the nearest Lazen had been to anything like a real relationship with a woman, perhaps the closest he could get. He desired her, but was blocked, paralyzed. James pictured him kneeling over her, gazing down at the bitter eyed disappointment and his flaccid, useless appendage. Had he ever emotionally faced the fact that he *had* a cock? He pictured her raising herself from the bed and pulling the strip of flesh between his legs, saying *fare l'amore con me* and Lazen, with the fear of that awful thing between her legs, unaware of her comforting him and saying that it was alright, that it really didn't matter, it wouldn't affect them. And holding him and rocking him as she would a child, 'There, there, *mia bambino*. I shall dance for you downstairs.' But he never watched her dance downstairs.

He thought of his own bedroom fiasco. He could see only Hanna's bowed head and not the prancing bravado of her misbegotten, revengeful sexuality. He felt bruised still, but was aware that his thoughts of and pity for his client had asserted themselves first, however temporarily.

As he walked he sent her a text asking if she was alright. It felt a little pathetic. He wished he hadn't; he'd even used the 'r u' abbreviation. He also rang Lazen. As usual, there was just a ringing tone. He walked through to the far entrance of the park then halfway back to his hotel before catching a bus for the rest of the journey. In his room he looked out of a window at a vivid sunset and idly realised that the curved corner of the building in early silhouette was the Coliseum.

CHAPTER SIX

His slough of intermittent sleeping and waking ended with an early morning knock on his door. He guessed who it was, hoped it was. He hurriedly put on a shirt and jeans and opened it. The brave smile was belied by the resignation in the eyes. He asked her in.

'It's okay,' she said in a low voice, 'I'm going to breakfast. And... I'm sorry.'

'So am I, I shouldn't have left you yesterday.'

She turned away along the corridor. 'Yes you should.'

He quickly finished dressing and went down after her. There were few residents in the room; she sat by a window table looking out. He seated himself opposite her.

'I've booked a flight.' she said, without looking at him. 'I'm going home today.'

'So am I, book me on the same flight.'

He told her he'd seen Luca again and that Lazen had gone. He didn't tell her why he thought he had. He asked her what he could have meant by 'home'?'

'London.'

'Luca thought the same. Pity it's not a more exotic location. You sure he hasn't got a favourite hotel in the Bahamas?'

'I wouldn't go anyway.'

'I was kidding.'

'I guess it's not worth checking L'Angelique.'

'No point, they'd say he'd never stayed there.'

He leaned towards her. 'I need to say this. I wanted you yesterday. I have for a while. You know this. Let's try to forget it happened. '

'Can you?'

'Probably not, but it won't make any diff - '

'It probably will.' She took a phone out of her bag. 'I'll try to get you on the same flight as me.' She used it and told him they'd be on the same plane. They left the table separately to pack their bags.

CHAPTER 7

She was several seats in front of him on the flight back to London. They spoke only little on the metro to Fiumicino and during the short wait before boarding. As they rose and banked he looked down from his window seat into a smoggy dusk beginning to be pierced faintly by the city's lights. He looked across and along the aisle and could see her pony tail and the back of her high necked sweater; she looked so upright and young. Their seating allocation felt symbolically appropriate.

As it grew darker and the night clouds became night he eased back in his chair and looked around him. He saw a woman breast feeding a baby, both child and mother sharing pleasure, becoming sated. He mused on whether female penis envy was an implicit conspiracy by men to hide their unconscious envy of the womb and woman's ability to create and sustain life. A cultural influence, of course, in that in a male dominated world while it's acceptable for a woman to want what a man has, the reverse doesn't hold. He stopped himself, took a deep breath and attempted to focus only on his client; for he was, he assumed, still that.

Dragging up his experiences with and knowledge of those few people he'd attempted to help that had similar symptoms and problems as Lazen, he tried to think rationally. His intuition then exploded this away and he knew with certainty that Lazen's earlier trauma, the original one, was that he had felt that his mother was destroying him at the moment of his birth, thus his slipping into unreality, a defence mechanism that had lasted all of his life.

His first image of the world, then, wouldn't be that of a smiling, loving Madonna, but a thing, an inimical object, and no matter how much love his mother would have given him throughout his childhood and beyond he would not really have felt it. And any future pain, virtually any pain, would be magnified and remind the child in him, the child that he was locked into, of that previous pain. It would be unconscious, it would take him over. In effect, he would *be* the pain. Any unfriendly situation or experience would be perceived by the child as hostile and the unreality would cement itself. But the pain of his unreal, acted existence could and probably had now become almost as great as the seminal experience he had pushed away. And his father? An alien presence that had detached him from the world even further by calling him 'son,' never by his name, turning him into a role, objectifying him. He could relate to people perhaps only intellectually and through escapist humour and theatricality. He must at times, thought James, despite his crying need, see all people as hostile objects. He wanted to tell Lazen these things, knowing that he would intellectually grasp there import and maybe, just maybe over the years find a real him, a self, a real world.

A full moon appeared silvering a cloud's edge; one outlined shape was the back of Lazen's head, another, his foot as it lifted from the ground. James began feeling a slow grip of anxiety some while before the aircraft rolled along the runway at City Airport.

They went silently through customs as a pale dawn was breaking, Hannah refusing to stop for anything, saying instead that she was going home to Aylesbury. He offered to accompany her to Marylebone Station. She refused.

'When can I see you again?'

'I need to be on my own.'

'At least you didn't say you need space.'

'Your pedantry gets in the way sometimes; you switch conversations to hat level so you don't have to feel what's being said.'

'Maybe. Listen, when you've done your thinking, let's - '

'Let me ring you'

''Don't call me, I'll call you?''

'Yes. Why do you want to ring me, anyway?'

'This is so unfortunate. It need not have happened. I know I only met you through my job, but, you've got to meet somebody somewhere.'

'Fatalistic determinism?'

'You sound like me.'

'I've picked up things. I wish you success with your job.'

'Can't we separate us from my patient?'

'Can *you* divide yourself from him?'

'Sorry, I'm making this worse. Take away the extraneous stuff and we'd have enjoyed it, yes? We'd have - '

'We can't. 'The moving finger writes and, having writ, moves on; nor all thy piety nor wit... ''

'That seems so bizarre.'

'What, when walking onto a platform at an east London station?'

An early train came in. He told her he'd travel to Bank with her. They got on, with James unsure whether this was just institutionalised banter between them denoting a familiarity he longed to extend or whether she was reluctantly filling the gap before beginning the recuperative time she wanted away from him. He stepped out of the carriage as its doors were closing, turned and silently mouthed, 'Ring me.'

As he stood there watching the back end of the train move further away he wondered whether, because he'd seen that inward, muted look of finality, been cowardly or for her sake had been brave enough to put her before himself. He knew it was the former.

He decided to take comforting refuge in a childhood bus ride through Silvertown, where bittersweet smoke from Tate and Lyle and the stale ale smell of Unilever had wiped away the sun long before Docklands dust had swirled and settled. He knew that his industrial background of women's headscarves knotted high on foreheads, henna'd hair, shoulder pads, aunt Lil smiling down at him before her and Sid's evening drink in The Plough; that time of double-breasted suits, roll ups, uncle Albert's pencil 'tash and flash of a gold tooth smile was all part of the underlying reasons for his attraction to Hannah. She represented tree-lined streets, bookshops, awning'd restaurants and parents that talked in abstractions, of ideas and not mundanely of the concrete and the personal. She had, he thought, probably sung in her church choir, too.

The journey was neither comfort nor refuge; he recognised only bits of cityscape: the terraced streets running away from the brown cliff of the sugar factory, a stretch of rusted rails that had run the goods trains, the curve of a Thames tributary, but not the Prêt a Manger where Terry's Cafe used to be nor Canning Town's bright red tower block.

On a train to Stratford before catching another one home and hearing the tinnitus tutting from ipods and smelling the odorous reek of noodles and vinegar'd chips, he idly pondered on whether there was an inverse relationship between increasing technological development and regression to the primitive. We'd become savages with smart phones.

The pile of letters his front door pushed into he flicked away with his foot before going into the study. The books on the shelves seemed sterile; they were just... there, as were his desk, Tiffany lamp and his old sofa, still smelling of leather. He opened the window to let in some air and noticed the leaves on his tree were beginning to turn yellow and brown. Not bothering to unpack he lay on the couch, closed his eyes and thought of his client again, mostly about their early meetings and the scenarios he'd watched, but in his case, playing the role of an actor playing roles, perhaps, even, another infinite regress like the virtually uninterrupted, eternal observing of himself. And if he was forever playing the role of what he wasn't, then was what he was merely another role? Perhaps we are all condemned to mean something, not be it. But then, his patient hadn't yet reached the stage of actually *being* what he was.

He was tired. Sometimes he would take the stairs, as he often did at train stations, two at a time, simply because he could. Now, he felt like crawling up them. As he fell into sleep still trying to prise away the feeling of a dawning pre-knowledge that Hannah wouldn't be contacting him again, he realised that he still hadn't written a word for Morgan.

He rang three patients the next day to tell them that he was back and booked appointments for two of them, the other saying that he didn't want to see him anymore. James wasn't sure whether this meant that he felt he didn't need a therapist or that he didn't want to see him in particular and was going elsewhere. Both were pluses, as long as, if it was the latter, whoever he saw could do better than he had. He also wrote a page of stilted, distancing jargon from his psychological lexicon for Morgan and put it away to re-write later.

Walking back to the station from a friend's flat in Stoke Newington the following day where he'd been cooked a lunch in return for proofreading his host's second poetry collection, his mobile rang.

'Hello, Mister Kent. How's Mister Kent then, eh? How's Mister Kent?' Lazen's voice had a loud, spoof joviality. He then repeated what he'd said, heavily stressing his listener's name. James asked him where he was.

'Oh, I'm just walking into Highgate Cemetery at the moment. Nice place, Mister Kent, lots of bushes and trees and, would you believe, graves and gravestones, too.'

'Why are you there?'

'Why? Why? Notice the rhetorical question here. Because I'm going to kill my fuckin' god, my *ex* god.'

'Your god.'

'Yes, my one; mine. I don't want it any more; I'm going to smash it. I have a hammer, I bought it, I hope it's strong enough, don't you?' His voice was growing louder. James imagined him marching through the cemetery, fists pumping.

'Exactly what are you going to destroy?'

'Did you not hear? A god.

'What god? *Can* you destroy a god?'

Lazen almost shrieked. 'Well, *I* can.'

James felt the first prick of fear for him. 'What exactly are you intending to do?'

'Smash. Smash.'

Rule number one: if a patient threatens violence calmly ask them why and express understanding of and sympathy with their answer.

'Do you think you could tell me why?'

'I didn't tell you, did I.' The voice was strained, the sarcasm still there, he sounded a little drunk. 'I found a god, or thought I had, worthy of being a god, someone who would have recognised me. He would, I know he would.' He was shouting again. 'But he wasn't a god. He was wrong, wrong, wrong, there can be no

CHAPTER SEVEN

socialist Utopia.' There was a long pause. James, in order to concentrate better, stepped into the doorway of a boarded up shop.

'Karl Heinrich Marx, eh? D'you think it's coincidence I have he same first name? A little bit of the unconscious again, eh, Mister Kent? It really is all economism, isn't it; it's too simplistic, and how can history have a goal? It's not testable, refutable, falsifiable. This transformation of the superstructure, this coming social revolution, this utter nonsense. And his view of human nature's so fuckin' naïve that - '

'Why not try Freud then, a very different model of man: not social, co-operative and, somehow, good, but lazy, hedonistic, self seeking, competitive; left to ourselves we'd have a Hobbesian war of all against all.'

James tried to remain calm, be as articulate as he could. He wanted Lazen to consider alternative gods - better to continue that fantasy, that wanting, than the yelling hatred and sense of loss that inhabited him now - but guessed that, for Lazen, it would mean little more than patronisingly crude banter.

'Yes, man is like that, but *he* got it wrong, too, he underemphasised the power of the mother, did he not? And where's the actual evidence for his beliefs?'

James left the doorway and continued walking. 'Thought much about existentialism? There's a certain - '

'What will that do for me? I can't find recognition in the Absurd. You're going to suggest somebody else next, are you?' The sarcasm had returned. 'Let's try Darwin, Mister Kent. We're told of the survival of the fittest, yet when asked how we know they're the fittest, we're told it's because they've survived. Tautology. What about a belief system; maths, going to offer me that?' He was shouting again. 'Beautiful, but it tells us nothing of the existence of things, does it. Where are you going from here, then?' Nietzsche? Wittgenstein?'

James knew the rule was pointless. He needed now to remind Lazen again that there can, of course, be no god, not for him, he'd eventually, as he had, despite his need for one, intellectualize it away. He had internalized the overarching theoretical framework of Marx as an all embracing, all knowing super narrative, a cohesive response to his own chaotic, inimical internal world. But its creator wasn't a supra human deity, some sort of pure god, a cosmic, floating intellectuality, but human, fallible. Lazen had been let down; a crutch had broken under him.

'If only we could,' he said in a quieter tone, 'suspend all judgements about the existence of the world and actions within it, perhaps push away knowledge of it or what we see as knowledge, to attempt to look afresh; epoche.'

'What does that word mean?'

'You must know what it means, you *must.*' He almost screamed it.

The phone went dead again.

James was worried now; thinking that this fake man who had lived a false life may harm himself. He started hurrying then running towards the station. He visualized a relevant train map, but couldn't quite pinpoint the nearest station to the cemetery and knew, anyway, he would have to change trains two or three times to get to it. He crossed a main road and turned away from the station entrance towards a nearby mini cab office and breathlessly asked when the next cab would be available. One had just pulled in. He got in the back seat and told the driver where he wanted to go; even then, as they moved off, noticing the dragonfly wing fanlight of a Georgian house as part of him tried to push the situation away.

His mobile rang. 'I can see it now. I can see his head, that granite lump. Shall I give you a running commentary?' Lazen began speaking in the voice of a race commentator. 'Well, here we are, it's a perfect day for it, the sun's just come out of a cloud, and it's hitting the trees behind the bust and there's a shaft of light striking the side of the face, the beard's glowing. The tall man's entering the straight now and moving towards it. He's taking the hammer from a bag which he's just dropped into a litter bin, keep Britain tidy and all that, and he's now less than a furlong from the finish ready to smash. And yes, yes, here he is in front of it.'

James could hear shuffling sounds followed by silence, then loud, clanging thuds. He asked the driver to hurry. He heard Lazen scream, '*Li mortacci tua,* mother fucker, *cago en la leche de tu madre,*' and in between the curses, the sharp, splitting,

CHAPTER SEVEN

crunching sounds of the hammer.

James pictured him reaching up and savagely smashing his tool at the bust, chips of stone flying off, maybe cracking it, but not destroying it; he'd need a sledgehammer for that. Perhaps he hadn't brought one because, though unaware, the child in him was frightened of some sort of punishment if he actually did destroy his god. But, in effect, Lazen was trying to obliterate the thing he felt had tried to deny his existence just as it had begun to exist. And somewhere in his head was his father's phallus.

The driver told him that they weren't far away. Two minutes later James left the vehicle before it had quite stopped. He went through the east entrance of the cemetery, fumbled for the fee and walked a few paces before he realised he had no idea where the tomb was. He turned back and asked an attendant. He ran; it seemed so inappropriate in a cemetery. It was a large place; he could see no one and hear only the drone of traffic and a distant train.

He could see from sixty metres away that the head had been attacked: a large piece was missing from the top, the side of the face concaved. But, no Lazen. He'd lost him again. He should have told him that he was coming to him, to stay there, that it would be okay. Why hadn't he? Stepping onto the low railing'd path leading to the monument he saw wedges and chippings of stone on the ground in front of him. Using his foot he dragged them into small piles before picking up some loose red flowers from the base, shaking particles of stone from them without knowing why. He looked up at the bust on top of the high tombstone. Lazen was tall, but not tall enough to have reached up and done what he'd just done. He couldn't have climbed up, either. James looked about him, the place seemed deserted still, but in the long grass behind a nearby grave was a small metal ladder and, not far away, some rag, wire brush and a spray can. There must have been a workman recently cleaning a tomb or gravestone and Lazen had used his ladder, throwing it from him afterwards.

James began walking away then turned. Taking a last look at the scene he felt for a second that it hadn't really happened and that if he was to turn around then back again all would be as it had been for sixty years; pristine and complete. Lazen had tried to substitute an ideal, something that can only be inferred, with a material entity, a human. Of course he had failed; his need had betrayed itself. James left the same way he had entered, thinking briefly of his glimpse of a tomb a few yards from Marx, a smaller one commemorating the sociologist Herbert Spencer; an ideological irony with a retail twist that would have amused Lazen.

He made his way to Highgate Hill and slowly down it towards Archway Station. It was only when he'd reached the bottom of the escalator that he understood the announcement that had been cackling distortedly from the platform speakers for some minutes.

'We are sorry for the delay to the next scheduled Northern Line train to High Barnet; this is due to there being one under at Highgate Station.'

He had heard it before; that casual, flippant, cruel piece of restricted code that signalled desperate death. He, like others around him, felt the twinge of annoyance at the disruption of a taken for granted expectation. Then a sudden conviction that the subject of the words that, again, were being repeated, was his patient. He sat on a platform seat while the people around him were deciding either to leave or impatiently wait. He put his head in his hands. Lazen filled him.

The man had had to face the loss of a god that never was, perhaps confront the terror of his birth and the shield of unreality his mind had cloaked itself in. James tried to imagine the self estrangement, the utter alienation of self and of it all crashing into his scarred psyche; and the panic that had made him run to a station platform and throw himself down. Did he scream? At last, an unobserved primal scream before the train obliterated it. Or had he watched himself watching himself as he stood on the platform's edge, caught in that infinite observational regress? Had he died in a wilderness of mirrors?

He left the station and walked towards the one at Holloway Road, thinking of Durkheim's societal reasons for Egoistical suicide, 'A prolonged sense of not belonging, of not having a tether, an absence that can give rise to meaninglessness and melancholy... the individual becomes increasingly detached from other members of his community.' The difference here was that Lazen had never been attached, except to an umbilical cord.

Dwelling on what he'd heard and seen during the last two hours he travelled a stop past his station. Interrupting his walk back was a call from a client who had been to his house an hour before and had impatiently paced the nearby streets wondering why there had been no answer to her knocking. He reminded himself that he had a practice to run, other clients; three potential ones had contacted him via his website during the last two days. He hadn't rung them, hadn't felt like it. He thought of a patient he'd been treating almost since the start of his practice who had last come to him six weeks previously and who James hadn't heard from since. On that occasion he was seeing him out after his session when another client had walked up the front path before his set time. James mentioned to the one who was leaving how talented the new arrival was; writing and composing songs and being effortlessly musical. James had then found himself striding to his gate and shouting at the back of his oldest and most insecure patient, 'I didn't mean you weren't clever as well, John, you are, you know that.' It shouldn't have happened. He wanted to call Hanna and tell her....what? That he missed her? Wanted her? That Lazen had thrown himself under a train? He went to bed feeling exhausted.

Morgan emailed him next morning asking if he was ever going to submit a progress report on the man he was providing funds to have researched; perhaps using him as an interesting example of whatever psychological category or categories James had bracketed him in and why. He knew he wasn't playing fair by Morgan. He'd been asked to send something each week so he'd know James' thoughts on his client and what had been happening. Should he tell him that he thought Lazen had killed himself and that, by definition, the project had failed? Perhaps he could write a paper for the British Journal of Psychoanalysts, 'A Client for 20 Days: Intimacy with a Suicide.' He was tempted to return the funds. He'd given back nothing. And there was, as ever, the implicit problem with his job, anyway: the paucity, like historicity but more so, of empirical data from the past, especially, for James, the impossibility of knowing the ontology of a client's womb experience, something that many psychologists ignored. He decided to compromise and subtract the cost of travelling to Paris and Rome and back and return what he'd received to date; Lazen's money meant he could afford to do so. He would also write a few pages for him.

Next day he went to Hampstead, ostensibly for a walk on the Heath and around Belsize Park, but covertly to buy a copy of the local newspaper. On page 2 was a photo of the partially destroyed bust along with an account by a young couple who'd witnessed some of the destruction. A tall, well built man standing on a ladder had been hammering at the tomb. He hadn't stayed long. He'd jumped down and run away. The writer thought it, 'undoubtedly the work of a political zealot.' On the facing page was a short report of an unknown man hit by a train at a local station. Two people, apparently in a state of shock, had been taken to the Royal Free Hospital for a few hours as a precaution. Perhaps Lazen hadn't carried credit cards and his mobile had been mangled. But who would report him missing, anyway? Gradia, maybe, and possibly Luca, who would be surprised though not worried if his comrade didn't turn up at the protest in Livorno. He may have rung him, but, getting nothing, would have assumed he'd changed his number; Lazen was like that. He'd mentioned to James a few hotels he favoured, but the latter doubted if they would reveal that he was in any of them; the L'Angelique, perhaps, being just one piece in a pattern of unrevealing.

James rang Luca anyway. He hadn't heard from Lazen and wondered if James had, though if he did miss the Livorno demo, there'd be a next one somewhere, possibly in Rome. James asked him what Lazen had thought of Marx. Luca laughed. 'Sort of worshipped him, really, he could do no wrong. Again I am working Mister Kent; I need to get back to it. Thanks for ringing. *Ciao.*'

It dawned on him that it was he who could, possibly, give a name to the man, if it was his client. But he didn't want to, didn't want to look at him. There were others who should do this. But he was the nearest. He rang the main police station in Hampstead and told someone that he was concerned about a patient he was to

CHAPTER SEVEN

meet at the train station the day of the incident - he could hear the euphemism to soften a violent death. After a wait he was put through to a Detective Sergeant who told him there had been some sort of fire under the front carriage of the train making identification of the person impossible. 'One of those rare occasions where the capture of DNA samples had not been possible, I'm afraid.' James tried not to visualize the roasted, incinerated lumps. He decided to leave things as they were; to leave well alone.

A few days afterwards, a time in which several new clients contacted him, either being referred by a doctor, fellow therapist or recommended by a former patient, he dredged up the courage to call Hannah. He was momentarily lifted when she answered; knowing it was him she needn't have. The feeling didn't last long. After his, 'Hello, it's me,' she said, in a strong, even tone,

'James, I'm sorry, but, though of course I hope you're alright and I wish you well, I don't think you should contact me again. Goodbye.'

She said it as if it had been rehearsed. He'd been expecting something like it, though perhaps not quite so final. A wisp of a thought occurred to him that she hadn't enquired after Lazen.

He received a letter an hour later from Morgan, Bayer and Partners informing him that they were disappointed. The few pages he had sent them hardly warranted the travelling costs incurred. Perhaps, it continued, it wasn't exactly his fault and that he had, possibly, needed more time with their client on a one-to-one basis to conclude his findings. They had taken a while to consider the rather scant nature of the material concerning what he'd found and the events so sketchily described and decided o take the matter no further.

Jams knew that, unofficially, they would. His standing in the profession would be damaged, possibly for ever. It had all been so unsatisfactory; the last three weeks had done little to convince him to work hard in the pursuance of his craft or on his reputation amongst its practitioners. At this moment, however, he didn't care, though deciding he would, perhaps, keep away from professional conferences and seminars for some time.

On his way to a Covent Garden cinema to see an afternoon matinee he called at 'The Croissant' in Wanstead for a coffee and saw Fabian. He recognised James immediately and shook his hand. He had opened two days previously and the place was busy. In between serving customers he excitedly told James that he was going to rename the place, 'Fab Bakery' and asked if he wanted to help choose the wall paintings. James declined; the enthusiasm for a majestic shot of Les Invalides or a view from the Sacre-Coeur, wasn't really there.

It was a recently released French film he'd wanted to see and he went in knowing it had already begun. There was a scene that only the French seemed able to do successfully: a married couple, on a whim, dancing in their living room, impromptu, familiar, swaying very slowly and continuing with nothing more happening, but showing an effortless truth. The action moved to London for a while then back to Paris. He saw a telephone box and a girl running towards it and knew immediately who it was; he'd had no idea that this was the film she was in. There were five minutes or so of action he didn't quite understand the significance of, then it seemed as if the director had, half way through the filming, realised how the camera seemed to love her and given his bit part English actor a more pivotal role.

There was a profile close-up of her staring across a stretch of water with a tear on her cheek; this time he didn't look for the camera's reflection. Then a static shot from the front, face looking sad as she drove along a road; the upward, arcing angle of tree tops not lessening the intensity, He wondered what was supposed to have happened to her; the brother dying, a lover lost, a sick friend maybe. But he knew that soon the scene would end and she'd get out of the car, technicians take the camera off the bonnet and, perhaps, the unit director smile and brush her cheek as the chief grip laughingly drove the car away. She'd then, maybe, light a cigarette, yawn and tell a stunt man jokingly to piss off. And all the time that first shot of her face was flooding his mind and he wanted to be with her, just with her, looking across the water.

She disappeared for a few scenes, again set in London, then back to Paris, but this time there were almost gratuitously

CHAPTER SEVEN

personal close shots; the camera moving slowly towards a diamond halter around her throat - he wondered if this was Lazen's present - an ear, a nostril, her lips, stopping, he felt, just short of penetration. He got up from his seat and left, feeling uneasy, as if she'd been treated like an object, a thing to be consumed; when, of course, it was he who wished to do the consuming.

On his way home, having a desire to do something ordinary and familiar, he collected a jacket from the local drycleaners, went into the house and rang his bank to check his balance. There'd been another payment from Lazen. Was he paying from the grave? He phoned and told them to cancel it and to tell the paying bank to stop payments, not giving a reason why. As he replaced the phone on the book shelf there was a metallic clang from his front door which signalled the arrival of something through his letter flap. He picked up a letter addressed to him and went through to the kitchen. Inside the envelope was a plain white card with, 'Thank you for trying' scrolled elegantly and familiarly across it. He looked again at the envelope. Around the bottom rim of the circular post mark was the word, 'Aylesbury.' He absently placed his jacket on a work surface and noticed a faded receipt from a Paris café sticking out of a pocket.

Pulling a kitchen stool towards him he sat heavily down. The room seemed dark and empty. He looked at the window, seeing the tree though it, its branches almost bare. Was Lazen staging another script, another *canovaccio,* was he tired of his global productions and was now taking them on a tour of the Home Counties? Had his other performers served as merely auditions and he'd now chosen his star for a permanent run? The mayhem in the cemetery was real enough, wasn't it? He could, just could have destroyed the awful genesis of it all; that huge, lacerating coming into the world. Perhaps, somehow, he had, in that one emotional crescendo, now, finally, been psychologically born. Was it possible? James had had patients for years that never got anywhere near that moment.

Had that fragmented self stopped watching other pieces of it, a self that slowly and painfully was becoming a whole? Was Lazen now real; a child in a man's body equipped with language, money, that undamaged intellect and, to the infant, a real mother now, Hannah, one to play with, pretend and fantasise with: You can be Peter with Flopsy and Mopsy, Karl, Postman Pat, Mr. Clever or Toby the Tank Engine, Charlie in the Chocolate factory or an aristocrat picking up a waitress, a flashy chancer with a beauty queen... He was alive. Lazen was living.

James sat there, numb, not an analytical thought in his head. He got off his stool and automatically began running water in the sink to wash up the breakfast plates. He watched it slowly fill, the swirling water sounding louder than usual, the plates knocking against each other. He picked one up, then another. He heard himself shout, 'Well, this is real, Lazen, you bastard.' and threw them simultaneously onto the tiled floor and stamped on their sharp, pointed, triangular segments as the splitting explosion filled his senses. He opened a cupboard, grabbed a bowl and slammed it against the wall. He looked down at the ceramic smithereens, one larger piece near the angle of wall and cooker rocking slowly to a stop. As he watched it, the words, 'Physician heal thyself,' boomed biblically inside his head,

Lightning Source UK Ltd.
Milton Keynes UK
UKOW02f1919221015

261195UK00001BA/138/P